NIGHTLAND

By the same author:

The Midnight Clowns
Rattlesnake and Other Tales (for adults)

NIGHTLAND

Robert Dodds

Andersen Press • London

First published in 2002 by
Andersen Press Limited,
20 Vauxhall Bridge Road, London SWI 2SA
www.andersenpress.co.uk

British Library Cataloguing in Publication Data available
ISBN 1 84270 081 2

Typeset by FiSH Books, London WC1
Printed and bound in Great Britain by the Guernsey Press
Company Limited, Guernsey, Channel Islands

Contents

For Jane Waygood

1
Aidan

It was morning break, and the boys in Claire's class were hurrying with tense excited faces towards the back of the sports block. There, a long windowless wall was the only witness to those little acts of school existence which were not for adult eyes. It wasn't just the usual band of secret smokers who were heading that way, it was *all* the boys, so Claire assumed it must be a fight.

'Who is it?' Claire said to Ronnie Whalen as he jostled past her.

Ronnie's breath made a grey cloud in the cold November air.

'Bobser and that new Irish kid in 8L.'

He grinned, and hurried on.

Claire's friend Katy caught her up.

'What is it?' she said, winding her long red scarf around her like a mummy's bandages.

'Bobser as usual.'

'Who's he picking on now?'

'The new Irish boy.'

'Aidan?'

'I don't know. Is that his name?'

'Yes. Aidan McCaffrey.'

'How do you know?'

Katy's mouth and nose were now under the scarf, but she arched an eyebrow expressively.

'He's cute!' came a muffled voice. 'I asked Holly in 8L who he was. I hope Bobser doesn't hurt him too much. He makes me sick.'

'Product of a broken home,' Claire pointed out, in fairness to Bobser. Apparently his mum had run off when he was little, and he lived with his dad, who he always referred to as 'the Hefay', whatever that was. Bobser was half Spanish.

'Serves him right. He probably broke it in the first place. Don't make excuses for him, Claire. He's a bully.'

'Do you want to see?'

Claire sort of hoped Katy wouldn't, but she did.

'Might as well. Come on.'

They joined the mixed group of boys and girls at the corner of the sports block. Further along was a tight circle of boys only, shouting and whistling. You could only glimpse Bobser and his fair-haired opponent occasionally in their midst. That was enough for Claire. She hated it when the boys had a fight, which wasn't very often, fortunately. But somehow she always felt drawn to watch them from a distance.

However, it wasn't long before Mr Rowan and Mr McEwen came galloping cavalry-style around the corner. Not for the first time, Claire glanced up to see if there were hidden surveillance cameras somewhere. There weren't. Teachers just seemed to be able to scent trouble. Like sharks.

The group at the corner, as innocent bystanders, stayed put. The circle of boys around the fighters however, implicated in the crime, scattered guiltily. Bobser and Aidan were revealed, still trading blows, oblivious to the disturbance. Mr Rowan bellowed like a bull.

'Stop that fighting at once! Do you hear me? Stop it *now*!'

Then Mr Rowan, red-faced and scowling, and Mr McEwen, all bustling goodwill and propitiating smiles, were into the ring like referees, pulling the combatants apart.

The scattered boys set up a ripple of hand-clapping as Bobser and Aidan were led away in invisible chains.

Claire studied Aidan as he walked past. He was tall, although not as tall as Bobser, and had wavy blond hair which he wore a little longer than most of the boys. His eyes were a pale blue and his jaw was set at a defiant, unbowed angle. Katy nudged Claire's elbow and giggled a little under her scarf.

'Look at Bobser, Claire! He's got a bloody nose!'

After this incident had brought Aidan to her notice, Claire found herself vaguely looking out for him at school. Usually she was deeply involved in some gossiping or mucking about with Katy and the rest of their gang. But she glanced around occasionally to see what Aidan might be doing. Sometimes he joined the other boys in their endless games of football. Bobser was always at the centre of these games, but he didn't seem to bother Aidan any more. She had the impression that he was accepted by the other boys but that he hadn't really formed any particular friendships. Often he hung about on his own, wandering around the playground and field with his hands in his pockets. It was impossible to tell if he was happy or not.

One day he looked up unexpectedly when she was observing him, and their eyes met. Claire was on her own, heading towards the tuck shop where the rest of her friends had gathered. Aidan had been walking the other way. To Claire's surprise and confusion he smiled, then stuck his tongue out. Feeling herself blush, she gave him the benefit of her special gargoyle face, the one she used when she wanted to give her younger brother Ben a fright.

Aidan had an excellent answer to that one, bugging out his eyes like a frog, pulling the corners of his mouth outwards and downwards, and letting his tongue loll out. He looked like a boxer dog abandoned by its owner.

Claire laughed.

'What's your name?' Aidan said. 'Miss Ugly?'

'Ugly yourself!' Claire replied, and moved on. It wasn't a great retort, but it would have to do. She couldn't risk hanging about long enough for Katy and the rest to spot her talking to Aidan. They'd tease her to death.

'Mine's Aidan!' he called out after her. She glanced back. He was smiling again. She gave him a little wave and carried on.

*

They started smiling shyly at each other after that, when their paths crossed. One day, a week later, Aidan was sitting on a wall that Claire walked past every day on her way home from school. She was on her own, so she slowed down and looked towards him.

'All right there?' Aidan said as she drew level.

Claire stopped.

'Yes thank you.'

'So what *is* your name then?'

'Claire.'

'Pleased to make your acquaintance, Claire.' Aidan held out his hand in a mock formal gesture and she shook it. His hand was warm, and grasped hers firmly.

'The boys and the girls seem to keep apart at this school,' he observed. 'Wasn't like that back home. I used to like talking to the girls. Some of them, anyway.'

Claire looked cautiously up and down the street. He was right about their school. At least, the early secondary years. In the junior department the boys and girls mixed together, and so did the older teenagers. But most of the twelve and thirteen-year-olds seemed to stay fiercely and exclusively in their own groups. She didn't want to be seen breaking the unwritten rules.

'Why's that then?' he went on. 'Don't you *like* boys, Claire?'

Claire felt a blush coming. How incredibly stupid. But it wouldn't stop.

'Yes. I do,' she said, 'but...I don't know...none of my good friends are boys.'

'Why's that then?'

'I don't know. It just happens that way. I stick to my pals.'

'And you're scared stiff they might come along the road now and see us talking. Aren't you now?'

'No.'

But he was nodding his head sagely, like a psychiatrist in some film. 'Oh yes. That's it. You're scared of what they'd say now.'

'I'm *not*!'

'Oh yes.'

Claire decided it was time to change the subject.

'Where are you from? Where were you at school before this?'

Aidan jerked his head over his left shoulder. 'Over there – over the water. Near Cork in Ireland.'

'Was that in a city?'

'No. Countryside.'

'So – what did you do . . . I mean, were there shops?'

'*Shops!*' Adrian's voice expressed a mixture of horror and disdain. 'What would I be wanting with shops?'

Claire struggled with this alien concept. Shops were her idea of heaven. And her friends' too. She tried another topic.

'Do you have brothers and sisters?'

'No. Only child. What about you?'

'A brother.' She expressed with a grimace that this was a misfortune. 'What music do you like?' she tried.

'All sorts.'

Claire reeled off a few of her favourite bands and singers. Aidan nodded noncommittally. 'Oh, they're all all right. I play my own music mostly.'

'Yeah? What do you play?'

'The harp.'

Claire goggled at him. 'The *harp*?'

'Yes. What's wrong with that then?'

'Nothing. No. It's just that . . . '

'You've probably never heard harp music, have you now?'

Claire racked her brains. Little angels sitting on clouds were lurking in there, playing harps. But she couldn't hear the sound they made. She shook her head.

'It's a popular thing in Ireland there. You think I'm a bit weird, don't you?'

There was something about Aidan's directness that made Claire uncomfortable. She shook her head again.

'Well. Maybe I am. Anyway . . . ' He jumped off the wall. 'I'm away to walk home now. I thought maybe I'd sit on this wall, from time to time. When it's not raining, you know. And maybe I'd see you here as you walked by. From time to time.'

Claire smiled. 'Okay. Can't stop you, can I?'

2
A Peculiar Thing

Aidan wasn't at the wall every day. But he was there quite often, and Claire took to hanging back slightly after the end of school bell, to avoid any possibility of having to walk home with Ben, her younger brother. She didn't need him running around the school telling everyone she'd got a boyfriend. Fortunately Ben preferred walking home without her anyway, so he never waited.

Aidan was an unpredictable conversationalist. Claire could see why he slightly unsettled the other boys, and continued to be on the fringe of their groups, without special friends. He was interested in such unusual topics, and jumped sideways from one to another so frequently that you found yourself struggling to keep up sometimes. His talk revolved around strange things he'd read in the newspapers about alien abductions, or Irish myths of transformations, or whether or not the Minotaur ever really existed. Sometimes he seemed to be half living in a fantasy world, and when they talked about books he revealed that he'd read *The Hobbit* and *The Lord of the Rings* several times each.

His fascination with mythical other worlds amused Claire, but what really appealed to her was that he was a good listener too. He was always ready to hear about all her friends and their fights and reconciliations, and the details of their sleep-overs or shopping trips, and contribute his own observations. In fact he seemed genuinely interested in *people*. Being new, and slightly excluded, had also made him an acute observer of the school which Claire had taken for granted all her life.

'The teachers now, they're more into keeping their distance here, I'd say,' Aidan said, when they were discussing differences between Ireland and England. 'Back home, they were more like friends of the family or something, or relatives even. They all had their own little qualities, and they weren't shy about letting their guard down.'

'Like how?' Claire asked. She was sitting beside him on the wall, as she usually did now.

'Well, there was Mr Sweeney for example. Hair the colour of tomato ketchup. Freckles like you've never seen. The most red-haired orange-speckled Irishman in the world. And he was twenty-five, he told us, and it was time he had a wife he said. So he joined some computer dating thing and told us all about the ladies he met. He never told us their names, but he told us everything else. As far as was decent.'

'What did he teach?'

'Oh, this was in domestic science.'

'*Cookery?* You had a man teaching you cookery?'

'Sure we did. He made a mean Irish Stew, Mr Sweeney. And a great Murghi Lamb with Ginger. That's another thing. We don't get domestic science in this school. That's a shame.'

'Yes. I'd like to learn to cook properly. Mum usually puts things in the microwave.'

'My mum does sometimes, but she still does some of the old traditional Irish dishes too. Pizza. Spaghetti Bolognese. Chilli con Carne – what are you laughing for? All those dishes originated in Ireland! The Italians stole them!'

'Chilli con Carne isn't from Italy.'

'Well – that's what I'm telling you. They're all Irish.'

'Oh yeah!'

'Anyway. I've got to go now. I want to do a little bicycle maintenance before teatime.' Aidan jumped off the wall and stretched. 'I'm doing a bit of cycling at the moment, you see.'

'When? You don't cycle to school.'

'No. At night. I go cycling at night. After dark.'

'You're having me on again, Aidan. You just make stuff up to see whether I'll fall for it, don't you?'

His face took on a pained expression.

'Would I do that, Claire? Lie to my best girl?'

Then he was off, and Claire wondered what the expression 'my best girl' meant.

For a couple of days Claire didn't see him on her way home, but around the school she noticed he looked pale and silent, and didn't join in the football at all. On the third day he was sitting on the wall, and looked as white as a piece of paper.

10

'What's the matter with you?' Claire said, studying his face. 'Are you ill?'

Aidan smiled broadly. 'I'm not ill at all. I'm just tired. It's all the cycling at night.'

'What? Come on – are you serious, Aidan?'

He nodded. 'It's true. But I can't tell you everything. You'd just think I was making it all up.'

'Well – try me.'

'No. I can do better than that. I can *show* you!'

'Show me what?'

'You've got a bike, haven't you?'

'Yes.'

'Could you get out one night with it, and meet me?'

'I don't know. When? What time?'

'It has to be late. When your parents are in bed.'

'Why?'

'Well, would they let you go cycling in the dark with me earlier on?'

Claire thought about it for a moment. She couldn't imagine the suggestion being well received.

'I doubt it.'

'There then. But it has to be late anyway, when everywhere's gone quiet. It has to be at midnight.'

'You want me to sneak out of my house at midnight and come cycling with you?'

'Yes.'

'You're mad.'

'But will you do it?'

Claire got down off the wall. She didn't feel like

11

talking any more this evening. She felt annoyed with Aidan for asking such a peculiar thing. And annoyed with herself because she wanted to say yes.

'I'll think about it,' she said, and walked off.

3
Cycling in the Dark

It was half past eleven on a Tuesday night, and Claire had heard Mum and Dad go chuntering up the stairs to bed about twenty minutes ago. Ben's gentle snoring drifted to her ears through his open bedroom door and, as always, the sound made her think of a little black pot-bellied pig. When she was little, and Mum and Dad told her there was a new baby on the way, she had secretly hoped it would actually be a pot-bellied pig. Ben had been a disappointment ever since.

'Claire is now sitting on the edge of her bed and putting on a tee-shirt and fleece. Now she is standing up and getting into jeans.' Claire commentated quietly on her own actions as if they were happening in some wildlife documentary on television. The whole scenario struck her as ridiculous.

She crept downstairs as quietly as a creeper, and slipped on her trainers. Then she opened the front door, which creaked alarmingly in the silent hall. She peered out. There was a slight halo of yellow mist around the street lights. The air felt cold and moist. She almost shut the door again straight away, it looked so uninviting out there.

But Aidan would be waiting. On the corner of Beech

Road, near the school. He would be looking up the street, checking his watch. She *had* to go. With great reluctance Claire pulled the house door shut behind her. If only she could be back in her cosy bed!

'Claire continues to act like a complete idiot,' she muttered as she made her way to her bike. It was kept under the steps leading up to the front door. She undid the padlock and wheeled it to the gate. Looking up and down the road, she was relieved to see that there was no one about.

Pedalling towards Beech Road, Claire stuck to the pavement in case any cars came along. She didn't want anyone to see her. The empty windows of the houses were black eyes that watched her go by. They looked like shocked faces, those comfortable suburban house fronts. 'Where are you going, a girl who's barely thirteen, at this time of night?' they seemed to be saying in scandalised tones.

Her pedals creaked a little. They added their opinion, in Claire's head. 'Stupid... stupid... stupid...!' The little dynamo that powered her lights whirred softly. 'Ssssssilly girl! Ssssssilly girl!' An owl hooted somewhere. Claire's imagination didn't reach as far as owl language, but she was sure it disapproved.

She reached the corner of Beech Road, after slowing down twice and being on the point of turning back and going home. Around the corner would be Aidan. She turned the corner.

Where was he? The long straight line of Beech Road

vanished into the mist. It was deserted. She straddled her bike and breathed heavily, a surge of anger and embarrassment starting to gather in her chest. He wasn't here! It was all a stupid joke, this bike riding in the night! She'd been had!

'Boo!'

A hand landed on her shoulder, and she stifled a scream. She turned, and Aidan was grinning like a monkey.

'Got you there, didn't I?' he said.

'Aidan!' Claire hissed. 'You idiot! You scared me to death!'

'Oh, sorry. It was just my little joke,' Aidan said, looking crestfallen. 'You were late, so I thought I'd hide behind the hedge here and give you a surprise.'

'Well it wasn't the sort of surprise I like! This is bad enough without you acting like a prat!'

Aidan nodded. 'You're right, Claire. I stand corrected. I will eliminate prat behaviour from now onwards. Forgive me?'

He smiled at her, eyebrows raised in mute appeal for mercy. Claire found herself smiling back. She wished she could stay angry for a little bit longer, but she couldn't.

'Anyway,' he went on, 'are you all ready for the riding now? Is your bicycle in peak condition there? I thought I heard some squeaking as you came along.'

'The pedals squeak a bit,' Claire admitted.

'Oh well. I suppose it doesn't matter as long as they go round. Come on then!'

Aidan slung a lanky leg over his bike.

'Where are we going?' Claire asked.

'That's for you to find out. First of all we go along Beech Road here.'

He set off at an easy pace, and Claire cycled along just behind him. They went to the end of Beech Road, passing the school gates, and then Aidan turned right onto Crows Wood Lane. This was a surprise.

'There's no street lights along here!' Claire protested. 'And this road just goes off into the middle of nowhere anyway. Right out of town.'

'Trust me!' Aidan grinned over his shoulder. 'It *does* go somewhere!'

Crows Wood Lane was not one of those roads that slink out of town furtively, with a fringe of straggling houses to disguise their exit. Instead, it immediately *was* a country lane, with no transition at all. No street lights. No buildings. Just a high thorny leafless hedgerow on either side and a swift embrace of darkness and isolation.

Once beyond the reach of the street lights on Beech Road, what had been only a slight mistiness gathered itself up into a thoroughly thick murky fog. Aidan was cycling faster, and Claire pedalled hard to keep within a few metres of his rear lamp. If she fell just a little behind, the bright red circle grew faint and threatened to disappear altogether.

'Aidan!' she called out, her voice enfeebled by the moist marshmallow fog. 'Don't go too fast!'

She could hear him call out something in response, but the words were lost, like stones dropped into a deep pool. He seemed to be cycling faster and faster.

'Aidan!' Claire protested again. Her legs were starting to ache, and the squeaking of her pedals sounded like a giant mouse running alongside her. 'Squeak! Squeak! Squeak!' its breathing laboured with the effort of keeping up the pace.

Aidan called back again. It might have been 'I don't care!' or it might have been 'Nearly there!' In any case, he was going faster and faster all the time. Reluctantly Claire pedalled her hardest to keep up. Before she knew it, they had passed an invisible and sudden crest on the road, and they were on a slope. A steep slope. The wheels raced around, and Claire couldn't pedal fast enough to keep up. She freewheeled. The road grew steeper and steeper. Moisture and fallen leaves glistened on its treacherous dark surface. They were going too fast. The hedgerows were a blur. If she touched her brakes now, she'd skid helplessly out of control. The foggy air rushing into her face made her eyes fill with tears. She tried to blink them away, but couldn't. She felt utterly panic-stricken. A disaster was inevitable. At any moment she'd be flying over her handlebars into the hedge, her limbs snapping like twigs! Bloody Aidan and his stupid bloody bike ride! Bloody, bloody, bloody hell!

'Aida...a...a...a...n!' she screamed, whether in anger or despair she couldn't have said. But her cry trailed behind her like a streamer of sound from a

17

skyrocket, and Aidan, up ahead, couldn't possibly hear her. But she could hear him.

'. . . the bridge!' she heard. 'Look out . . . bump . . . ' she heard. Then she was flying through the air across a hump-backed little bridge over a dark river. She glimpsed murky water flowing beneath her, like black ink. She heard the sound of rippling and gurgling against the stones of the bridge, like a voice. Then, miraculously, she thumped back to the ground and started to slow down as the road ascended a gradual slope beyond the river. As she ran out of steam, she found herself pulling abreast of Aidan who had stopped to wait for her.

'You think that was funny I suppose!' she gasped out. She was shaking all over.

'Now, don't get cross, Claire! We had to go fast to get here. Look up ahead!' Aidan said excitedly, his face dripping with fog moisture. Following his pointing finger, Claire could see a dazzling silvery light penetrating the murk in front of them.

'We're here!' Aidan said. 'Now you'll see! Just up this next slope!'

Before she could reply, he pushed hard on his pedals again. She quelled her exasperation and did the same. A minute later they reached the top of the rise and burst out of the fog together as if smashing through a physical wall. There, swimming in and out of focus in her watering eyes, was a dazzling moonlit landscape.

'The Nightland!' Aidan said exultantly.

4
Nightland

Claire had never imagined that moonlight could be dazzling. But hanging in the sky ahead of them was a huge brilliant disc which you couldn't look at directly. Below, bathed in silvery light, was a vast panorama. Her eyes travelled across the scene, but her brain failed to make any sense of what she was seeing. This was a wild landscape of forests and mountains, dotted with steep-roofed little villages and lonely towers. A long way off, a huge waterfall fell silently in a sinuous line from a distant craggy ridge. Far, far away, on the edge of vision, was a glittering flat sheet of frosted light that could only have been an ocean.

'How did we get here?' she said, unable to turn away from the magical scene.

'It's a mystery,' Aidan said. 'It happens the same way every time. You go faster and faster until you go across that river, and then you're here.'

'But ... in the daytime ... there's no waterfall ... and we're nowhere near the sea.'

'I've been along Crows Wood Lane in the daytime. There's no hill, no bridge, no river. It just goes across fields for a couple of miles until it joins the main Barchester road at a T-junction.'

'So...'

'So we're not in our own country any more. This is the Nightland. It's all different. Come on, you'll see.'

Claire hesitated.

'Aidan – this is so weird. Are we dreaming?'

'I don't think so.'

'Is this place safe?'

'I've come to no harm. Come on! It's fun, honestly! You'll love it!'

They coasted slowly down the gentle incline ahead. Dark yew trees lined either side of the road, their dense forms bent over them like watching giants as they passed. The surface of the road was covered in a grey floating mist, only a few centimetres deep, so that they seemed to be cycling down a stream with their bicycle wheels half submerged in water.

'There's a bit of a surprise up ahead,' Aidan said, half turning. 'But don't be frightened.'

'What sort of a surprise?' Claire said apprehensively.

'Well, you like animals, don't you?'

'Ye...es.'

'Just think of it as an animal, like any other. I've got a bit of cake in my pocket for it.'

Claire tried nervously to see beyond Aidan on the road ahead. They seemed to be heading into a dense wood of yew trees. They grew taller and taller over the road, their branches now blotting out the moonlight, creating dense pools of shadow. There was a deep silence all around them, broken only by the squeaking of

Claire's pedals. Eventually the road stopped going downwards, and they were on level ground, surrounded on all sides by trees.

For perhaps five minutes they cycled on through the dark silent wood. Then Aidan stopped, and Claire brought her bicycle to a halt beside him. Up ahead were two enormous trees bending towards each other to form a kind of gateway. Through the gap, Claire could see that they were at the edge of the wood, and moonlit fields lay beyond.

'What are we waiting for?' she asked Aidan, who was fumbling in his pocket.

He brought out a little parcel of tin foil, and started to open it.

'Ssh! You'll see. Just don't be frightened.'

'I *wouldn't* be frightened if you didn't keep saying "don't be frightened"! What do you need cake...'

Claire was interrupted by a sound in the distance. In the deep silence of the wood, a dog barked. No, not one dog. A number of dogs, barking in unison. All barking together, at exactly the same time. That was unnerving. How could the dogs all bark at exactly the same moment like that?

'Ah...here he comes!' Aidan said. 'Now remember, he's just a big softy.'

The barking grew louder, as the dogs approached. It didn't sound like friendly barking to Claire. She put her foot on her pedal, ready for flight if necessary. There was a rustling noise in the undergrowth as whatever it

21

was got closer. Then, bounding through the tree trunks towards them came a furry bristling vigorous shape. A dog of some kind, very big. As big as a Saint Bernard. But on its thick neck were three heads!

Claire grabbed Aidan's arm in alarm. 'What's this thing?' she squeaked hoarsely.

'Ssh! Don't worry.'

The creature had slowed down, and was now stalking towards them inch by inch. The middle head was barking loudly and menacingly. It looked like a huge angry alsatian. On its left, barking in a friendly kind of way, was the head of a black labrador. And on the other side, yapping irritably, was the head of a Yorkshire terrier.

It came to within about five metres of them and stopped suspiciously. Aidan threw a piece of sponge cake onto the ground in front of it.

'Here we are then, boy! Cake!'

The barking stopped immediately, and the three-headed dog nosed its way towards the cake. The black labrador head bent down eagerly to gobble up the treat, but was angrily jerked away by the alsatian. Unfortunately for the alsatian though, it jerked too far, allowing the little Yorkshire terrier head to grab the cake.

Aidan threw down more pieces of cake, and all the heads managed to get some in the end, although not without a lot of growling and squabbling. Then the dog padded forward and allowed its heads to be patted. It only had one tail, but that was wagging hard enough for three dogs.

Claire leaned forward and patted each head in turn nervously.

'The first time I came here, this fellow wouldn't let me get past him,' Aidan said. 'I got to this wood, and he stood barring the way out to the fields. So the next time I brought him some cake, and he let me go past. Now then, boy! Goodbye for now!'

The strange beast stood aside as they cycled on into the moon-bathed fields. Glancing back, Claire saw it snuffling hopefully on the ground for crumbs.

As they came right out of the trees into the full moonlight for the first time, Claire became aware of a beautiful warmth suffusing her body.

'It's warm! The moonlight is like the sun!' she exclaimed to Aidan. 'Stop a minute!'

She took off her fleece and stuffed it into her saddle-bag. The bare skin of her forearms gleamed white, like bleached bone.

Some of the fields were filled with glistening silvery wheat loaded with kernels of grain. In others bearded barley was growing, the stalks sagging like tired old men whose heads are too heavy for their thin bodies to carry around any longer. Away in the distance, a line of figures was moving along one of the fields, waist deep in the rich crop, wielding scythes.

'It's harvest time here,' Aidan said. 'Every time I've come they've been cutting down the grain. But the funny thing is, the fields are still full of the ripe crops. It's as if more springs up as soon as one lot is harvested.'

'Have you spoken to any of the reapers?' Claire asked.

'You can't. Come and see.'

Aidan veered off the road onto a rutted track across the fields, towards the line of workers. Claire followed. As they got closer, the figures seemed to become faint and insubstantial, as if they were made up of a fine mist. At last, when they had approached to within a few metres, they disappeared altogether. Aidan stopped and looked at Claire.

'Wraiths, you see. They just vanish into thin air.'

'But who *are* they?'

'I couldn't say. Look behind when we cycle back to the road.'

They headed back the way they had come, and sure enough, as Claire glanced back over her shoulders, there was the line of wraiths again, working as hard as ever cutting down the corn.

'They're scary,' Claire said.

'Well, they seem to be harmless though. This country is full of them. What's more, I don't think *they* can see us either. There's a village up ahead. See what you think.'

5
Donny and Jake

The lane they were following zig-zagged through fields until, rounding a corner where an old willow stood admiring its reflection in a reedy pond, they came to the edge of a village.

'Who lives here?' Claire said.

'More shadow people. You can see some of them at the lit-up windows of the cottages.'

'Are they like the reapers in the fields?'

'They seem to be. The doors of the houses are usually unlocked, and if you go in, the people vanish.'

The streets of the village were narrow and twisting and the higgledy-piggledy houses leaned over them as they cycled through. At some of the windows were flickering yellow candles and, in the rooms behind, Claire could sometimes glimpse the people of that place. They were eating, reading, talking, stoking the fire. There were children playing or getting ready for bed. At one window an old woman with a kindly face looked out.

She reminded Claire of her grandmother, who died when she was only six, and on an impulse she waved at her. But the old woman didn't seem to see her.

'Who can all these people be?' Claire said.

'I don't know,' Aidan replied. 'But do you notice they

25

don't seem to have any modern things in their homes? I mean, there are no television sets or computers. They seem to be living in the past.'

'Perhaps they're ghosts?' Claire said.

'I thought that at first myself. But then ghosts are usually in our world, aren't they? And here, we're in *their* world, and they can't see us. So does that make us the ghosts?'

Claire mulled over that thought as they cycled slowly onwards. She didn't much like the idea that she'd become a ghost.

They came to a small green at the centre of the village. There was an old stone drinking trough there and a sagging wooden bench.

Beside the green was a big ramshackle building with yellow gleaming lights shining out of its many diamond-paned windows. 'The Ship Inn,' Aidan said, pointing up at the pub sign. A full-sailed galleon was pictured in a valley of deep waves. From inside came a sound that could have been a crowd of noisy drinkers, or could have been waves crashing onto rocks.

'Take a look inside,' suggested Aidan.

They leaned their bikes against the trough and Claire walked fearfully towards the door of the pub. Looking in, she involuntarily grasped the door frame to steady herself. Inside, everything was pitching and tossing back and forth as if on a ship at sea. The bar was filled with noisy drinkers holding pewter mugs. They were mostly men, wearing old-fashioned sailing clothes – fishermen's smocks and bell-bottomed trousers. Many of them had long wagging beards. They stood with legs wide apart, braced against the floor as it surged backwards and forwards. Tankards were hung from nails in the beams above their heads, and clanked and clinked together in regular waves.

Claire backed away and for a moment or two the whole village around her rolled around. She felt as if she'd just stepped ashore off a boat.

'Not called "the ship" for nothing, is it!' Aidan grinned.

Just then, over Aidan's shoulder, Claire caught a glimpse of movement. She stared. Coming across the green towards them, flying recklessly across the grassy humps and hollows, were two boys on mountain bikes. They wore tee-shirts, shorts and trainers and baseball caps, and looked as far out of place in this ancient village as Aidan and herself. She started to say something to Aidan, but a shout interrupted her.

'G'day, mate!' The boy's voice had a broad Australian twang. 'Brought your girlfriend I see!'

Aidan turned around as they came skidding to a stop.

'Hi, guys! This is Claire. Claire, this is Donny and that's his brother Jake. They're from Wonga Bonga or somewhere like that. Middle of nowhere.'

'Pleased to meet you, Claire. How old are you?'

Claire found her hand being shaken vigorously. Jake reached over and shook it too.

'How old? I'm just thirteen,' she said. Her head was

in a spin. Three-headed dogs. Ghostly reapers. Pubs that acted like ships at sea. And now Australians. What next?

'Struth! A teenager, Jake! You hear that? We're twins, Claire. Twelve years and ten months. Just hot on your heels. I'm the noisy one and he's the quiet one. He usually gets all the girls.'

The quiet one pulled a face.

'He makes it all up,' he said, jerking a thumb at his brother. 'I'm no quieter or noisier than he is, and neither of us gets the girls because there aren't any in Wonga Station. It's a sheep station, and there's only us and Mum and Dad and the shearers.'

The boys both tipped the peaks of their baseball hats upwards. Claire wondered if they acted in unison deliberately or it just happened that way.

They both had open, smiling faces, and looked tanned and healthy even in the white light of Nightland's moon.

'But how did you get here? And how do you know Aidan?'

'Oh, we come here on our bikes, same as he does. There's a secret place.'

'Do you cross a river?'

'Yeah, we cross a river to come here. After midnight.'

'But your midnight would be the middle of the day for us, wouldn't it? How come you're here at the same time?'

Donny shrugged. 'Hadn't thought of that one, Claire. Struth, blowed if I know!'

28

Claire turned to Aidan. 'You didn't tell me there were real people here as well as the wraiths.'

'Well, there aren't. Only Donny and Jake.'

'Come on, mate! We're real!'

'No, that's not what I mean. I mean there's no one else, as far as I know. I've never met anyone else here from the outside, except Donny and Jake.'

'Our brother's here somewhere though,' Jake said.

'Your brother?' Claire said.

'Mikey. Four years older than us. We're looking for him.'

'How do you know he's here?'

'Told us, Claire,' Donny said. 'He told us he came to a special place in the night, but we never believed him. When we were little ankle-biters, he used to wind us up something rotten. Told us all kinds of tales. Then he disappeared. One night. So we knew where he was.'

'How long ago . . . ?'

Jake took up the story.

'This was about three years ago. It was terrible for Mum and Dad. They think he wandered off into the bush somewhere and just died of thirst. Everyone on the ranch searched all over the place for days, but they never found him.'

A chill breeze passed along the skin of Claire's arms, raising goose bumps.

'Your poor parents. But have you been looking for all that time?'

'Only found the way in last year. It's a big place,

29

Nightland – and you can't stay too long. This is your first visit, is it?'

'Yes.'

'Well, have you told her, Aidan, about getting back?'

'Not yet.'

'You've got to be out of here by moonset. When the moon goes down, Nightland goes completely dark. And that's when the Reapers come out.'

'The reapers? But they're out now, in the fields. Aidan and I went close to them and they just dissolved.'

'No. That's not them. They reap the corn. The Reapers of the darkness are harvesters of lives. They'll cut you down, if they can catch you.'

'But...'

'They cut you down, and then you'll stay here. You'll never return.'

'But how can you know any of this?'

'Mikey told us. Before he disappeared. He said he'd met people here who'd stayed too long. They warned him.'

'So, do you think these...Reapers...have caught your brother?'

'We don't know. It's possible. All we can do is come here and look for him, until the moon goes down.'

They were all silent for a moment. A sombre mood had descended on them, and Claire looked about her at the moon shadows of the houses, wondering if dark sinister figures were lurking there, just out of sight.

She looked at her own shadow, stretching thinly along the grass of the village green like a gaunt scarecrow. She waved her arm at it, but the shadow didn't move.

'Aidan . . .'

'What?'

'My shadow . . . it . . . it doesn't do what I do!'

Aidan waved his own arm and shrugged his shoulders.

'The shadows are strange here. They're dead things. They move around with you, but like you say, they don't move the way they should.'

Again Claire felt that cold suggestion of a breeze flickering icily across her skin.

'I . . . I'm not sure I want to stay any longer, Aidan.'

All the boys turned to her in some surprise. Donny smiled.

'Hey, guys! We've been spooking the poor girl with these stories. No, Claire, you're safe here for ages yet. Look – the moon's right up there, as high as she goes. No worries.'

'And you've hardly seen anything yet,' Aidan said with a grin. 'This place isn't so scary. It's fun. We'll show you some of the sights!'

Aidan and Claire remounted their bicycles and the four of them cycled out of the village. Very soon Claire found that they were on a long straight road with walls on either side of it. The walls were made of huge slabs of rough grey stone, too high to see over. After a while, they came to the back of a long queue of people, shuffling along at a slow but steady pace in the same direction as themselves.

'No need for us to join the queue,' Aidan said. 'We

can just go to the front.'

Claire glanced at the people's faces as they cycled past them. None of them was talking to any of their neighbours. Everyone seemed to be lost in their own thoughts. Some looked worried, others were serene. Some wore deep frowns of concentration, as if they were desperately trying to remember some important information they had been entrusted with. Many of the people were old, but not all of them. They seemed to be quite an international bunch as well. The village had been strange enough, but at least it had seemed faintly familiar – like a kind of old-fashioned English country place. But here was a long featureless road full of Chinese, Indians, Africans and all sorts of people whose origins she couldn't even guess at. What was going on?

'Who are these people?' she said to Aidan.

'More shadow people. They don't see or hear us, and look at this…' To Claire's horror, Aidan suddenly swooped sideways on his bike, straight towards the queue of people.

'Look out!' Claire shouted.

But there was no cause for alarm. The figures merely shimmered slightly as Aidan cycled through them, as if in a heat haze. It was as though they were just made out of air.

'You see?' Aidan smiled as he came back. 'They're just wraiths.'

Claire looked at the oblivious queue. 'I didn't like

that, Aidan. It didn't seem right.'

'What do you mean?'

'I just mean, it didn't feel as if you were treating them right, cycling through them as if they didn't even exist.'

Aidan looked thoughtful.

'I know what you mean, Claire. Sort of lacking respect?'

'Yes. I suppose so.'

'Yes. I only did it to show you what they were. I wouldn't do that otherwise.'

Now, in the distance, a large square building came slowly into view. First its roof, then gradually the whole thing, as if it were rising slowly out of the ground to meet them. The road ran straight up to it. As they got closer, Claire could see that it was made of the same rough grey stone as the walls beside the road. There were only two windows, great blank dark rectangles which watched their approach like a pair of eyes. The road went into a great gate, and above the gate was a carving of a pair of weighing scales. She couldn't think immediately what that meant, but Donny called over his shoulder, 'We call this place Kangaroo Court, Claire,' and she remembered that scales were the symbol of justice, the weighing of evidence, or of good and bad.

'So are all these people being put on trial?'

'You tell us!' Aidan said. 'We've been here a few times, but we still can't figure it out.'

6
The Court of Minos

They were now passing under the lintel of the gate. The road became a broad corridor as it entered the building, and the queue of wraiths thinned out as they made their way into various doorways and openings on either side of the main route. Some of these openings were rather strange. For example, there was a little hatch set into the wall at about two metres above the ground, and a number of wraiths were taking it in turn to try to haul themselves up to get through it. Most of them seemed to be too weak and frail to succeed, and eventually gave up and drifted on to another, more accessible exit. If they'd only co-operated, thought Claire, and organised a system of standing on each other's shoulders, then they could all have got in. As she watched, an unusually agile figure hauled himself up and through with apparent ease, watched enviously by the others below.

There didn't seem to be any obstacle in the way of simply proceeding straight ahead. At the far end of the building the moonlight shone through an exit doorway. But somehow all the people who entered the courthouse seemed to filter off one way or another, so the far door stood empty and unused.

'Where do they all go?' Claire said, as they

dismounted from their bicycles and leaned them against the wall. 'How can you have hundreds and hundreds of people coming into a building and none leaving it? Do they just dissolve?'

'Come and check it out,' Jake said, pointing to a doorway that seemed popular with the wraiths. It had a great wooden door on swinging hinges which creaked constantly as a steady stream of people pushed through it.

They mingled invisibly with the crowd, which obligingly melted away at their approach and re-formed slightly ahead and behind them. They were now in a narrower corridor which echoed with the whisper of shuffling feet.

Sure enough, the corridor led into a courtroom. Claire had never been into a courtroom in real life, but she'd seen enough courtroom dramas on television to feel completely familiar with the wooden panelled walls, the tables laden with huge leather-bound books, and the stern-looking gentleman in a white wig seated high up on a dais at the front of the room. But she looked in vain for a jury, or indeed any signs of a normal trial being conducted. As the wraiths filed down the central aisle towards the judge, he merely waved them onwards with a weary gesture, like a traffic policeman.

This was where it became impossible to follow the progress of the wraiths any further, because there was no exit from the courtroom. Instead, the line of people walked straight into the wall to one side of the judge and simply vanished.

'You see?' Aidan turned to Claire. 'Is this a trial or not? Are these people guilty or innocent?'

They sat down on the front bench (where the legal teams for the prosecution and defence should have been, Claire thought) and watched for a few minutes.

The judge was a very old man whose face looked as if it had been mercilessly pinched and tweaked into a state of blotchy redness. His cheeks burned like little fires, and his chin was sharp enough to slice bread. The lines on his face suggested a rather stern character, particularly two deep frown marks above his pointed nose. Although he appeared bored with his present activity, there was a twinkling light in his eyes that hinted at something livelier.

'Who do you suppose he is?' Claire whispered to Aidan.

'There's no need to whisper,' Aidan replied in a voice that bounced off the wooden-panelled walls. 'The old boy's only a wraith. He can't hear us. Deaf as a post.'

'Indeed, young man? And what makes you think the old boy's as deaf as a post, eh?'

Claire would have laughed if she hadn't been so startled. Aidan's hair had stood on end as if a jolt of electricity had run up his leg and into his head. His eyes were popping, and his jaw dropped open like a trap door. It was the first time Claire had seen him anything other than cool and collected.

'Wha... wha... wha...?' he said, or something like that.

The judge was looking straight at them, still motioning the wraiths onwards with one hand.

'Well? Enter the courtroom of Minos, and you must expect to be judged. So far, I am inclined to find you guilty. Guilty of making blundering assumptions without a shred of evidence. What do you have to say, young man?'

Amazingly, Aidan had recovered some of his self-composure.

'I beg your pardon, sir. I had no idea you could hear or see us. I've been here in your court before, sir, and you never showed a sign of noticing me.'

'Well, and why should I? You're not the first living mortal that's come blundering in here like a tourist. You'll be bringing your cameras and camcorders next and wanting souvenirs. On the whole, I find, it's best to ignore you all.'

'Did you say your name was Minos, sir?' Aidan went on.

'I might have done, or I might not. You should pay attention.'

'I beg your pardon. I... we... were wondering where all these people were going, and if you were, er... judging them, at all?'

'I don't answer questions. I ask them. What are you four mortals doing here?'

He turned his head slightly towards Donny and Jake, as if to remind them that they were in the same boat.

Donny cleared his throat. He looked scared.

'If it please your gracious worshipful sir, me and my twin brother Jake here are searching for our older brother Mikey, who disappeared down here some time ago.'

'What do you mean, *down here*? Did you fall down a hole to get here?'

'Er...no, your lordship.'

'Well don't talk nonsense then. I don't know anything about your brother. He hasn't been through my court-room. I remember everyone.'

This seemed hard to believe, as he had waved about fifty wraiths onwards through the front wall of the courtroom while he had been talking to them, and he hadn't glanced at them once.

'Could you offer us any advice?' Jake piped up.

'Advice? I'm not here to give advice. I'm a judge. The only advice I'm prepared to offer is that you should get out of here and back to your own little world before it's too late. Otherwise you *will* find yourselves under my judgment, or that of one of my fellow judges Rhadamanthus or Aeacus. And you might not like the verdict. Now go!'

They didn't need a second invitation to leave. The judge's eyes had turned a fiery red colour, redder than his cheeks, and the frown marks over his nose had deepened, so that his whole face now directed at them the most baleful threatening scowl imaginable.

They hurried back out into the main corridor, where they'd left the bikes, and looked at each other. Even Donny and Jake's sun-browned features were pale as death.

'Let's cycle out of the far door straight away,' Aidan said. 'That's the first time anyone's ever spoken to me in here.'

'Us too,' Jake said. 'Mikey said there were people here who could see you – including the Reapers of course. But we'd no idea the old judge could ever see us. We must have been in there half a dozen times without him letting on.'

'I wish he'd been more helpful,' Donny said. 'We might have asked him more questions.'

'That's amazing, Claire,' he went on, as they cycled through the now empty corridor towards the moonlit exit. 'Your first visit to Nightland, and you meet a talking wraith straight off!'

From the far side of the courthouse, there was an extensive view. Immediately in front of them, lush meadows sloped gradually down towards a river. The river was wide, much wider than the one Claire and Aidan had crossed to enter the Nightland, and it glittered in the moonlight like a living thing, a great silvery snake wriggling its way off into the far distance where, right on the edge of sight, lay the shimmering sea.

On the far side of the river, Claire could see a road. It was busy with moving figures: little dots of people, and larger objects that might have been wagons or carts or carriages. A long way down the river, perhaps half way to the guessed-at distance of the sea, stood a sight that stirred Claire's heart. It was a castle. A magnificent many-turreted castle with flags fluttering from every rooftop and pinnacle. Even at such a distance it looked magnificent.

'What's that castle?' she said to the others, pointing.

'We've never got that far,' Donny replied. 'It's a long way off.'

'And you'd have to get over the river, to get onto the road that goes to it,' Jake added.

Aidan was looking at the castle too, shading his eyes against the dazzling moonlight.

'It looks grand, doesn't it, Claire? I've thought before now that I'd like to see it up close.'

'It's too far,' Donny said.

'You've already said that,' Aidan replied. 'Your short-term memory's on its way out.'

'All right, cobber! Keep a civil tongue in your head!'

Aidan continued to look at the castle. 'I wonder if we *could* get there. If we came again to Nightland, Claire, and set off straight for it, cycling fast and not stopping for anything. I'm sure we could do it.'

'Count us out,' Donny said.

'We already had done,' Aidan replied.

Claire couldn't understand the sudden tension that seemed to have grown up between the boys. She remembered Aidan's fight with Bobser. Maybe boys found him too abrupt and, well, a bit bossy. Jake and Donny were certainly bristling now. They looked at each other and seemed to come to an instant unspoken agreement.

'Well, catch you later,' Donny said. 'We'll go and

have a gander round the back country before heading for home. Nice to meet you, Claire!'

'Yes. Nice to meet you too. 'Bye!'

The boys swung their bikes onto a path that went away to the right, away from the courthouse, and disappeared into a wood a few hundred metres away.

'What was all that about then?' Claire said.

'All what?' Aidan said, finally tearing his eyes away from the distant castle.

'Arguing about nothing with Donny and Jake.'

'We weren't arguing.'

'Yes you were. About whether it was possible to reach the castle.'

'Oh, they were just being wet blankets as usual. That's all.'

'What do you mean?'

'Well, just that they're a bit cautious. There's one or two times I've tried to get them to go down that way with me, towards the river, but they never will.'

'But they must have a reason...'

'Something their brother's supposed to have told them. Not to cross that river. But they could at least come down and look.'

'Have you ever gone down further – through these fields?'

'Yes. We've time to go down to the river now, if you want. There's something strange to see down that way.'

Claire laughed. It seemed such a redundant observation. 'There's something strange to see everywhere here! But have we got time?'

'Well...' Aidan looked up at the moon. It was high in the sky, but not as high as it had been earlier. 'It's hard to be sure...'

'Haven't you ever timed it?' Claire said. 'Don't you know how many hours you've spent in here?'

'Look at your watch.'

Claire looked at her watch. The hands stood at twelve o'clock exactly.

'Twelve midnight! But that's impossible. We came down Crows Wood Lane at midnight!'

'Outside time doesn't seem to move, when you're in here,' Aidan said. 'It'll still be midnight when we get back.'

Claire looked towards the river again. She wanted to see everything she could.

'Come on then, if you think there's time,' she said.

They coasted down the gently sloping road ahead. Wraith sheep bumbled about in the meadows, tearing at the grass and baaing softly. Near to the river, the ground flattened out. Here there were large numbers of wraiths gathered, a great silent crowd, all facing towards the river.

'Where have all these people come from?' Claire asked.

'Look behind you,' Aidan replied.

Looking back up the hill the way they had come, Claire could see the square silhouette of the courthouse at the top. In the fields beside the road, which had seemed empty except for the sheep as they passed them, wraiths were flocking down towards the river like autumn leaves falling from a tree.

'Where are they all going? Are these the same people as were in the courthouse?'

'I think they might be, but I'm not certain. But they're all coming to cross the river. Come and see.'

A few hundred metres along the river, the crowd was gathered more thickly. It was very strange to see so many people standing in complete silence. Their pale faces were staring intently at the river, and if they moved at all it was to take a small shuffling step nearer to the water.

On the far bank, Claire could now see more clearly the busy road that led, eventually, to the castle. Traffic was moving in both directions – people on foot, some with staffs or walking sticks, and wagons drawn by horses or oxen, heavily laden if they were travelling downstream, and usually empty if they were going upstream, away from the castle.

'Now – look, here's how we can get over the river, next time we come.'

Aidan pointed to the far bank, about fifty metres away. There was a wooden jetty there, sticking out into the water like a crooked, gnarled old finger. It sagged alarmingly in places, and the bent props which jutted out of the water to support it were green and slimy with water weed. As Claire watched, a long flat boat shot out into the stream from the far side of the jetty. Standing at the rear of the boat, and propelling it from a standing position with a single oar pointing down at a steep angle into the water, was an ancient-looking man with a long grey beard. He wore tattered robes that were probably once white, and looked like a Roman senator who had been rolling in the mud with a couple of dogs. His eyes were fixed on the bank ahead of him, and shone with a strange red light. Looking to her right, Claire now saw that on this bank too there was a jetty, where a line of people stood patiently waiting their turn for the ferryman.

The current in the river was obviously strong, for the ferryman steered his craft upstream, before gliding back down to berth at the jetty on their side. In spite of his obvious age, and scrawny appearance, he handled the boat with great ease.

Now, as they watched, about fifty people filed aboard the flat boat, where they stood upright, packed densely together.

'Do you see how the sides of the boat don't sink down into the water?' Aidan said, pointing. 'All those people getting aboard, but obviously they don't weigh anything at all!'

The ferryman had hopped ashore, and was using his long oar to chivvy his passengers along. When he judged that his boat was full, he gave a great whack on the arm to an old man who had just been about to climb aboard, and thrust him back. Then he climbed aboard himself, untied the rope that had been slipped around a post, and pushed the boat out into the river once again with a great shove on his oar against the end of the jetty. Again he held a course easily against the river's current, and steered across at an angle before drifting slightly downstream once more to moor at the opposite bank.

'Do you think he'd take us across?' Claire asked.

'Well, we can't go now. We've taken too long getting here. We'll come straight here next time.'

'But, I mean, will he take us anyway?'

'Oh, I see what you mean. Well, he probably won't see us, like most of the wraiths. Otherwise, I don't know. We'll have to talk our way on board.'

Aidan glanced upwards, then pointed.

'See, Claire? The moon's on its way down now. It's time we went.'

Claire looked up. The moon was behind the courthouse on the horizon, and the moon shadow of the building reached out like a long hand across the fields towards them.

They cycled slowly back up the long slope which had been so easy to descend until they reached the courthouse, and then took the path that Donny and Jake had followed into the woods. These were pine woods, and the dark track they followed was cushioned with pine needles.

'Why aren't we going the way we came?' Claire asked.

'This is a shorter way. Wait and see. We'll come this way next time, to get to the river quickly.'

The track went on and on, twisting this way and that, until Claire had no idea where they might be. Occasionally the trees parted and they cycled through a small clearing. The moon had sunk now below the level of the tops of the trees, and Claire began to find thoughts of the Reapers creeping into her mind. Aidan was cycling quickly, and when they shouted a few words back and forth, Claire thought she could detect a note of tension in his voice, as if he too was aware of some danger.

Finally the trees ended, and they cycled across an area of open cornfields towards another wood about a mile away. The moon's rim was resting on the horizon, like a silver coin balanced on its edge, ready to fall over.

'Is that the wood where we came in?' Claire called out. She was exhausted now, and as well as feeling scared, she felt angry that Aidan seemed to have misjudged their journey, and that they now had to be in such a panic to get out.

'Yes, that's it. Not far to go now.'

'Why didn't we leave earlier?'

'Not my fault. It's a tricky thing to judge. Sometimes the moonset seems to come more quickly than other times.'

They cycled into the wood. Somewhere, faint in the distance, there was the barking of dogs. However, they passed through the the wood without seeing the three-headed creature, and then puffed and panted their way up the path between the secretive yew trees to the top of the slope, where they paused briefly to catch their breath. This was the vantage point where Claire had first seen the Nightland, and now she looked back as the moon slipped lower. It looked as if it were impaled upon the sharp ridges and tips of the distant mountains.

'We've made it all right,' Aidan said, breathing heavily. 'I don't know how I got it wrong like that. I usually get back here before the moon touches the horizon. Anyway, come on. It's only a minute from here down to the bridge.'

They freewheeled down the steep slope ahead, into a shifting curtain of moist mist which prickled Claire's face and bare arms. They gathered speed, and once again Claire had that horrible feeling that she was going too fast, that she might skid and crash at any moment. Then, in a flash, the dark little river and the hump-backed bridge were there, immediately in front.

They shot across at top speed, tyres leaving the ground for a couple of seconds, then thumped down and gradually slowed to a halt on the far side, breathing hard.

Claire looked around her. There was no moon, but it was not completely dark. A wind rustled in the trees beside the road, and an owl hooted somewhere. Glancing back, there was no sign of the bridge or the river.

'Crows Wood Lane,' Aidan said, matter-of-factly. 'Welcome back to the boring real world.'

7
Something for the Ferryman

'Are you going to the Nightland again tonight?' Claire hissed at Aidan, without looking at him. She stopped and pretended to be looking at the sports notice-board so he had time to reply.

They were passing in a corridor between lessons. Aidan looked the way Claire felt. Death warmed up. White as chalk. He feigned an interest in the hockey results.

'Yes. Meet you at the same place?'

'Yes.'

It was all there was time for. Already Claire's friend Katy was waiting for her. She hurried to catch up.

'Chatting up Aidan McCaffrey? I didn't know you were on speaking terms.'

'We're not!' Claire said illogically, flushing pink.

'Not speaking! So what was that going on back there then? Miming?'

'Oh all right. We are on speaking terms. But it's nothing.'

'I wish you'd talk to him some time when I'm there. So I can join in. Will you?'

'If you like. He's not so interesting.'

Katy just looked her in the eye with an expression like

a wronged sheep until she couldn't help bursting out laughing.

On her way out of the house at midnight, Claire stumbled on the stairs. Some thoughtless adult had left a heap of laundry there. She heard her mother sit up in bed like a jack-in-the-box. The springs were noisy.

'What . . . what's going on?'

'Just me, Mum. Getting a drink of water from the kitchen.'

'Oh . . . mmm . . . all right.'

'Goodnight!'

There was a gentle subsiding of springs.

'Goodnight . . .'

Claire waited for five minutes by the clock in the kitchen before going quietly out of the front door. It was surprising how long five minutes took to pass in a cold dark kitchen, but you couldn't be too careful. Mum was a light sleeper. Unlike Dad, who would sleep through the Last Trump, snoring all the way.

Aidan was waiting for her at the corner of Beech Road. Tonight the sky was clear, and millions of stars were watching them.

Aidan pointed upwards.

'Amazing, isn't it, that we're looking into the past when we look at starlight.'

'Do you think we go to another planet, when we go to Nightland?' Claire asked Aidan.

'Don't be daft. Think how far away other planets are.'

Claire bridled.

'What's your theory then, Mr Know-All?'

'I don't have one. It just happens.'

'Magic?'

'I don't know. I don't need to know. It's enough that it happens.'

They set off towards Crows Wood Lane.

'Mankind would still be in the dark ages if there were more of your sort about,' Claire said. 'No scientific curiosity.'

'Maybe we are in the dark ages now. Thinking that science can explain everything. What sort of a daft idea is that?'

'Science *can* explain... well, most things,' Claire said, a little lamely.

'Well, I'll tell you what. I've tried a little scientific experiment of my own. I picked up a pine cone in the woods there in Nightland, and tried to bring it back with me.'

'And what happened?'

'Just vanished when I crossed the river. I had it in my hand, and it faded away like one of the wraith people when you approach them.'

'But *we* don't vanish when we go in there.'

'Ah – well. That got me wondering. Maybe we do. I mean, the wraith people can't see us, can they?'

'No...'

'So maybe it works both ways.'

'But we can still see *ourselves* there. And each other. And what about that judge?'

'Right enough. It's a great conundrum, as my old science teacher in Ireland used to say.'

'Do you think the wraith people can visit us?'

'I don't know. That could be what ghosts are, couldn't it? Visitors from Nightland.'

They turned into Crows Wood Lane. Claire remembered her terror last time, when she had been going too fast to control her bike.

'Can we take it a little slower this time, Aidan?' she said.

'No use. I tried that once as well. If you just potter along, you come to that T-junction with the Barchester road. No bridge. No Nightland. You've got to go as fast as you can.'

'I didn't like it.'

'You've got to sort of let go. Be reckless. Then it just happens. Come on!'

He pulled ahead of her, pedalling hard. Claire followed his lead. They went faster and faster until suddenly they were swooping down that precipitous slope that came from nowhere. This time, because the night was clear, Claire could see the river up ahead, black as oil. But beyond the bridge there was nothing. Just a sheet of darkness.

They flew across the bridge and up the slope on the other side. The sheet of darkness rippled like water when a stone has been thrown into it. Then they were on the top of the rise, and the glittering silvery vista of the Nightland lay before them. The moon was high, sailing almost directly overhead, like a great searchlight illuminating every corner and crevice of the lands below.

'Well, we should have hours of time on our side,' Aidan said, glancing upwards for a moment. The moon was too bright to look at for longer.

'Do you think it's the *same* moon as ours?' Claire said, squinting at it through a little gap in her fingers. 'With the Sea of Tranquillity and the Ocean of Storms and so on.'

'Are those on the moon?' Aidan said, looking surprised.

'Yes. They're not real water, of course.'

'I *know* that much! I just didn't know the names. I don't suppose it's the same moon. Or maybe it's the dark side, the side we never normally see. Come on, we haven't got time for astronomy if we're going to get to the castle!'

They cycled quickly through the wood. The three-headed dog came tearing after them out of the darkness, and Aidan threw a piece of cake for it without stopping. The little Yorkshire terrier head got the whole lot, so the labrador and the alsatian looked very put out – especially the alsatian. They left it squabbling crossly between the two huge trees which formed a leafy gateway out to the fields of corn beyond.

They cycled quickly through the fields, hardly glancing at the lines of labouring reapers whose harvest work never seemed to be done.

They cycled quickly along the winding path through the silent forest, with its deadening carpet of pine needles.

They cycled quickly past the back door of the courthouse, and down through the pastures to the lush water meadows beside the river.

Only then, when they were close to the jetty and the patiently waiting crowd of wraiths, did they stop and draw breath.

'I've...never...cycled...so hard in...my life!' Claire gasped out.

Aidan had a water bottle on his bike, and they took turns to gulp down a drink.

'It's worth it though. The moon's still right overhead, and we should be safe for ages. The next thing is to get across this river!'

They wheeled their bikes along the tottering jetty. The ferryman was half way across, heading towards their bank with an empty boat. The line of wraiths showed no sign of seeing Claire or Aidan.

But when the ferryman had brought his craft alongside the jetty, and slipped its dripping rope over the post at the end, there was no mistaking the look he directed towards them. He could see them as clear as day.

He took a dark bottle out of a small tattered bag that lay in the boat, and pulled out its cork with a resounding *thwump*! Putting it to his lips, he took a long swig, his red eyes never leaving them, before he re-corked it and put it back in the bag, smacking his lips and wiping his beard on the sleeve of his filthy robes.

'Now then, whippersnappers!' he said, having refreshed himself. 'What brings you to these parts?'

'We want to cross over the river, if we may, and visit the castle down the river,' Aidan replied.

'Cross the river!' the ferryman repeated, shaking his head as if unable to believe his ears. 'And visit the castle! Why would you want to do that?'

'To see what it's like. It looks so beautiful.'

The ferryman stroked the long straggling strands of his white beard.

'Ah, to see what it's like. You're curious, are you? And what did curiosity do to the cat?'

'Curiosity killed the cat,' Aidan replied. 'Are you advising us not to go?'

'Advising? No, not me. I never advise. I'll take you across. I've taken all sorts across here. But you'll have to pay me. You must pay the ferryman.'

'Pay you with what?'

'Have you no money about you? No coins?'

Aidan looked at Claire and shrugged his shoulders.

'I've never brought money here. I've never thought I'd have to pay for anything in the Nightland,' he said.

Claire shook her head. 'I haven't any money either.'

The ferryman looked at her with an expression of greed and cunning.

'Ah, but what's that on your wrist, my dear? Is that a bracelet?'

Claire was wearing a bracelet. A simple chain, with a little blue stone. It hadn't been expensive.

54

'Will you take that?'

'Oh yes. Bangles and baubles will do nicely for the old ferryman. He can buy his bread and wine with those.'

Claire unclasped the bracelet and dropped it into his outstretched palm, which closed around it like a venus flytrap shutting on a fly.

'Thank you, my dear. Climb aboard!'

Aidan started to lift his bicycle over the edge of the jetty. The ferryman cleared his throat and held up his hand.

'Ah...you were wanting the bicycles to go over as well, were you? Bicycles are extra.'

Aidan stared. 'Bicycles *extra*! Who makes up the rules here?'

'I do. Bicycles take up a lot of room.'

'Well, we haven't anything else to give you.'

The ferryman's red eyes drifted towards Claire.

'What's that around your neck, my dear? Is that a necklace?'

Claire flushed. She felt as if Aidan would be wondering why she'd put on so much finery for a trip to the Nightland. Why had she? Anyway, at least it was proving useful. Reluctantly she unclasped the necklace, a birthday present from Katy. It wasn't expensive either, but Katy would notice that she didn't wear it any more, and there'd be no point in telling her she'd given it to a ghostly ferryman in another world.

Again the ferryman's claw-like hand closed like a trap

on his booty. He chuckled cheerfully, a sound like water going down a drain.

'Come aboard then, whippersnappers, come aboard! I'll make a special trip for you!'

With that, he whacked with his oar at the wraiths who were crowding anxiously towards the boat.

'Get back! Get back! There's no hurry for you. These are express passengers, with no time to lose!'

'We'll want to come back across, later on,' Aidan said. 'You're not going to want more payment, are you?'

'No, no. Return ticket included.'

Then for some reason he cackled delightedly to himself.

They skimmed across the fast-flowing river at a surprising speed. The ferryman seemed in high spirits, and sang snatches of some incomprehensible song as he stirred his long oar in the water. At the far side he even helped to lift Claire's bike off the boat, revealing the same surprising wiry strength that his boatmanship displayed.

'How far is it now, to the castle?' Aidan asked, as the ferryman jumped back into his craft and slid away again.

'Far enough, but not as far as you think!' was all the reply he got, called out in a thin cracked voice above the bubbling splash of the river.

'What an irritating old man!' Aidan said to Claire, as they got onto their bikes and pushed off on the pedals for the last leg of their journey.

The road was bustling with activity. Horses drawing heavy carts piled high with mysterious bundles and

56

sacks plodded along the same way as they were going. Others, trotting more lightly, pulled empty carts in the opposite direction. Wraiths of all descriptions walked briskly along. Unlike the silent shuffling queue for the courthouse, many of them were in groups, seemingly talking with great animation, although not a sound could be heard. There seemed to be more people going towards the castle than coming away from it, but it was busy in both directions.

Every now and again they came across a great oval bronze plaque set into the paving of the road. The plaques seemed as old as the ancient paving stones of the road itself. Faint lettering, much faded and worn down, was just barely legible on their surfaces.

'*I will be a brother to my fellow man,*' Claire read out, when they stopped their bikes at the first of these. 'That's all very well for boys. What about *I will be a sister to my fellow woman*?'

Aidan shrugged his shoulders. 'That's a pretty vague sentiment anyway. What's it supposed to mean?'

The next plaque suggested *Neither a lender nor a borrower be*, and the next *Do not bite off more than it is possible to chew*.

'These are really annoying,' Claire concluded.

'They're not worth stopping to read, are they?' Aidan agreed. 'I can't see anyone else standing about reading them.'

So after these first three plaques, they cycled past the rest, although Claire glanced at each of them as they went by, and glimpsed odd snippets such as *boldly go, the hindmost,* and *paved with good intentions.*

For a long time they couldn't see the castle, but eventually they crested a slight rise in the road and got a good clear view. Now they were closer to it, they could appreciate its sheer size. It was more like a small mountain than a building. People and horses and carts milled about the huge entrance gates like ants scurrying in and out of their anthill.

'It's enormous!' Claire exclaimed.

As they got nearer, the road became a causeway, raised above a great flat marshland dotted with pale white flowers.

'They look like some sort of lilies,' Claire said, pointing.

'I couldn't identify a flower to save my life,' was all Aidan's response.

The causeway led like an arrow straight to the castle gates. The gleaming castle loomed over them, its ancient stonework blanched white by the moonlight, and the voices of the bustling wraiths could faintly be heard, like a collective whisper, so that a high 'Ssssssh...' sound reverberated against the cliff-like walls. Claire wished her pedals weren't squeaking. They seemed the loudest sound there.

'There's nothing to stop us going in, is there?' Aidan said, as they drew up to the gates and dismounted.

Claire glanced back behind them at the moon. It looked as high in the sky as before.

'Are you sure we've got time?'

'I think so. And anyway, we haven't come all this way just to see the castle gate, have we? I want to know what makes this place tick.'

Claire too felt a burning curiosity, now that they had come so far. This seemed the busiest place in all the Nightland, the beating heart of all that lay around them. In spite of her misgivings, she felt it would be stupid and just too pathetic to turn back now. So she nodded, and they leaned their bikes against the castle walls and walked in through the gates.

8
Dicie Ravenscroft

Beyond the castle gates they came into a great courtyard filled with people. Carts were being unloaded, and all kinds of mysterious packages being carried through a small doorway off to one side. Steaming horses were being brushed down and fed. Through a half-opened door Claire could see the rise and fall of a blacksmith's hammer, striking showers of sparks from an anvil. The muscular arms of the smith gleamed orange in the glow of the flames from his forge. There were wooden pens filled with pigs and chickens. There were soldiers leaning on their halberds, or directing people what to do. But the most striking thing about all this hustle and bustle was that it was almost soundless. It was as if you were watching a television programme with the sound turned right down. Even the blows from the smith's hammer only sounded like the tapping of a woodpecker on a distant tree.

Although Claire knew they were invisible, she couldn't help speaking in a bare whisper.

'Why's everyone so quiet do you think, Aidan?'

'I don't know. And do you get the feeling we've arrived in the Middle Ages somehow?'

They watched the goings-on for a few moments more, then Aidan pointed at something.

'Look – do you think that's the way in?'

At the far end of the courtyard was a flight of stone steps. This led up to an archway with double wooden doors swung back wide open. As they crossed the courtyard, the busy wraiths obligingly melted out of their way as soon as they got close to them. At the top of the steps, Claire noticed that the wooden doors had intricate carvings on them. They were not easy to discern clearly, as the moonlight didn't shine directly on them. They seemed to represent a lord and a lady in magnificent costumes. But both the lord and the lady were skeletons with great hollowed-out eyes.

'I don't like these much!' Claire commented.

'Not very welcoming,' Aidan agreed.

Inside, torches burned in black metal brackets along the walls of a wide passageway. Huge tapestries were partially illuminated by the flickering light. In contrast to the silent bustle outside, here there was no one to be seen at all.

Aidan started to stride along the passageway quickly, but Claire called him back.

'Hold on, Aidan! Look at this tapestry. Surely that's the courthouse!'

They both scrutinised the dimly lit woven scene. Sure enough, there was a great square building with a pair of scales over the entrance. But all the figures lining up to enter the building were skeletons.

'And this one here shows the village we were in, doesn't it?' Claire said, moving on to the next tapestry.

61

It did depict a village, and skeleton faces peered out of the windows of all the houses. But in the middle of the village, where the green and the Ship Inn had been, was instead a kind of whirlpool, in which a sailing ship crewed by terrified skeletons was being sucked under the waves.

'They're a bit creepy, aren't they?' Aidan commented, with a short laugh.

The laugh echoed coldly along the passageway.

The next tapestry also had a nautical theme. It showed a harbour where a magnificent sailing ship was setting sail. The usual mob of skeletons were on board. But further out to sea there seemed to be an identical ship, or perhaps the same ship at a different point in time. And this time the figures on board were clothed in flesh, and their faces wore expressions of joy.

'Come on,' Aidan said impatiently. 'These are all very interesting, but we've got to use our time to look around as much as we can.'

Claire followed him, glancing sideways at the tapestries as she went. She had the feeling that the stories they told were important to understanding the Nightland, but she didn't have the key that would unlock their full meaning.

At the end of the passageway there was another opening, and this led into a great banqueting hall. Long tables surrounded an open area in the centre, and on a slightly raised platform at one end was a table laid with silver dishes and goblets. Dozens of candles in silver holders cast their wavering reflections in the silverware.

'This is a posh place to have your dinner!' Aidan commented, picking up a goblet. 'Cheers, Claire! Your good health!'

Claire made a mock curtsy in reply, but she didn't feel in the mood for light-hearted joking.

There were several other doorways leading out of the hall, and they stood irresolute for a few moments, wondering which way to go. Just at that moment, a faint sound came drifting through the stone passageways to their ears. Aidan held up a hand.

'Listen, Claire ... it's a harp.'

They went to each doorway in turn and listened.

'This way, do you think?' Aidan said, at the third one. The notes of the harp could be heard more clearly, a little tinkling stream of sound in a distant stony place. They followed the notes up flagged steps, along corridors, around corners. Sometimes they were led into an empty room, sometimes along a long passage that ended only in an embrasure, a narrow window slit looking out across the moonlit marshes dotted with white flowers. Sometimes the music seemed to come from nearby, sometimes from an infinite distance. Sometimes above, sometimes below.

'This is driving me barmy!' Aidan said at last. 'Do you think this harpist is giving us the run around or what?'

'Could it be a wraith harp – you know, like the people here – just fading away when we get close?'

'Could be. Nothing would surprise me. Anyway, let's

just head back to the banqueting hall, shall we? There doesn't seem to be anybody in here, in spite of all the crowd in the courtyard.'

They retraced their steps and almost immediately came to a door half opened on their right. The sound of the harp came more than ever from inside.

'Did we pass this door on the way?' Claire asked.

'I don't remember it,' Aidan replied. 'Let's go in.'

It was a beautiful room, illuminated by moonlight streaming through two large archways. Beyond these was a balcony. Out there sat a girl of their own age with long silvery hair, playing the harp.

They walked up to the nearest archway and looked at the girl.

'It's lovely music,' Claire said to Aidan.

'Not a tune I know,' Aidan replied. 'She's not bad, but I would say she's not been playing the harp for all that long.'

The girl with the silvery white hair was beautiful, Claire thought, and it seemed to her that her fingers moved with the grace of dancers across the harp strings.

'No. She could do better if she had a good teacher,' Aidan went on.

The girl stopped playing abruptly and looked straight at them.

'*Well if you're so good, show me yourself, Mr Know-All!*' she said.

Claire clutched Aidan's arm in shock. They had both

assumed, of course, that this girl was a wraith, and would neither see nor hear their presence.

'I . . . er, I do beg your pardon!' Aidan said. 'I had no idea . . . '

'No. No idea at all!' the girl agreed, tossing her hair back petulantly. 'Blundering about here like a pair of elephants and setting yourselves up as music critics.'

'Well, if you want to know the truth,' Aidan said, recovering his wits, 'I think I *could* help you play better. You're not holding the harp the right way, and that means you can't reach all the strings with your fingers at the right angle. You're straining too much and it makes your touch too heavy on the lower notes.'

The girl looked slightly mollified. 'Really? I don't have a teacher any more, and I suppose I might have slipped into bad habits.'

'What's your name?' Claire said, coming forward.

'Dicie. Dicie Ravenscroft. What's yours?'

'Claire Swift.'

'And I'm Aidan McCaffrey.'

Dicie's eyes, pale icy blue, looked them over. Then she smiled.

'You've come at a good time. The King and Queen and everyone are out on a grand hunt, but they'll be back at moonset, and then you can join the feasting.'

'But – we can't stay until moonset!' Aidan exclaimed. 'Are you mad? We've got to get back before it goes dark.'

'Why?' said Dicie standing up and laying the harp

carefully against the stool she had been sitting on. She looked at Aidan. Her eyes were narrowed, penetrating.

'Why? Because no one stays in Nightland after the moon goes down.'

'I do.'

'*What?*'

'I said "I do". Nothing happens.'

'But it gets completely dark, doesn't it?'

'Yes. But the castle is ablaze with light. It's a wonderful time. The castle fills with people. I watch from this balcony, and they all come flooding in through the gates. It makes me think of moths coming out of the darkness towards a beautiful light. Then I go down to the banqueting hall, and we feast and play games and sing and dance. Why don't you stay and see for yourself?'

'I've never met anyone who's stayed in Nightland,' Aidan said, shaking his head. 'I thought it was dangerous.'

'Where are you from?' Claire asked.

'*From?* Oh, you mean from out there.' Dicie looked disgusted by the question. 'I'm from Oxbury, in England.'

Claire couldn't believe her ears. 'Oxbury? But that's where we're from! What school do you go to?'

'Greengates.'

'I don't know that school. Where is it?'

'On the Banford Road.'

'Oh...'

'So you cross over...' Aidan said, 'I mean, into Nightland...'

'On Crows Wood Lane. Is that where you come in?'

'Yes. I can't believe it!' Aidan scratched his ear. 'I'd no idea anyone else came that way. You came on your bicycle, did you?'

'Yes. It's down in the cellars somewhere. I've been here for ages.'

'But – hasn't anything happened to you?'

'No. I can go back if I want to. I just prefer it here, for now. There's no time passing outside while I'm here. I could just go back any time and it would be the same. Boring and . . . sad.'

'Aidan . . . we've got to go, haven't we?' Claire said, pointing at the moon. It had definitely begun its descent now.

He looked up at it. 'Yes. We've got a long ride.'

Dicie laughed. 'If you could see yourselves! All anxious about getting back! Stay! Join the feast! You can go back later. Do you think I'd lie to you?'

She smiled at them. It was indeed hard to disbelieve her. Aidan looked at Claire.

'What do you think?' he said. She could tell he was tempted. Dicie took a small step towards him. Claire felt a shiver go through her. She didn't like Dicie getting closer to Aidan.

'I think we should go, Aidan,' she said. 'Listen, we can always come back here again. We know the way, and we can cycle hard and spend longer with Dicie next time. Maybe bring Donny and Jake? I don't think we should stay now.'

67

Dicie ignored her. 'But I'd like to hear you play the harp, Aidan! Just so I know you're not deceiving me!'

Aidan looked at the harp, leaning against the stool out on the balcony.

'No...I think it's best we go now...'

All the same, he stayed rooted to the spot. He seemed to be searching for something else to say. Dicie came up and put a hand on his shoulder and took his other hand in hers.

'Do you know how to dance as well as play the harp?' she said.

'I can do an Irish jig I suppose,' Aidan said, a little embarrassed.

Dicie laughed and whirled away from him towards the balustrade of the balcony.

'Oh, that would do! An Irish jig! You should stay for the feasting!'

'Come *on*!' Claire took Aidan's elbow. 'We've got to go! Goodbye, Dicie!'

'Goodbye, Claire. Are you staying, Aidan?'

Aidan looked torn. Claire gave him a tug.

'No. No...not this time,' he said eventually. 'I'll come back tomorrow, I'll come back with more time to spare.'

Claire wondered why he said *I* and not *we*. Perhaps he just hadn't been thinking. And why had Dicie tried to separate them? She only seemed to want Aidan to stay. A surge of jealous irritation made Claire almost drag Aidan away from the balcony and through the room to the door. Dicie stood watching, leaning against the balustrade, the moon sinking in the sky behind her.

'I'll see you again, Aidan!' she called. 'Be sure to come!'

9
Caught Out!

It was nearly midnight on the next day. Claire felt very tired, but she'd exchanged a few words with Aidan at break time and he was determined to go back to Nightland tonight. She could have done with a night off herself, but she didn't want to let him down. Or else, perhaps, it was more that she didn't want him to go on his own. He seemed, if anything, more excited than ever. His face was as pale as a ghost's, and his eyes were like little flames burning in dark hollows.

'You need a rest,' she'd said to him, but he'd just shaken his head.

So, as carefully and quietly as ever, Claire slipped out of bed and got into her clothes. She drew aside her curtain a little and looked out. A murky, drizzly night. If only she could stay in bed!

She crept down the stairs like a mist floating over the ground. In the kitchen she stopped for a glass of milk. Then she went to the key caddy where all the household's keys were ranged neatly on little hooks. They were meticulously labelled in tiny writing by her dad, who liked that sort of thing. But the hook which usually held her bicycle padlock key was empty.

'Funny...' Claire muttered to herself. Perhaps she

had left the key in the lock last night. She hoped no passing bicycle thief had spotted it.

She took her house key and slipped out. There was her bicycle all right. But it was padlocked to her brother Ben's bike. Had she done that last night? She had been so tired she couldn't remember.

Anyway, it gave her a problem. She looked at her watch. Five to midnight. Aidan might be waiting already. She must have kept the key in her jeans pocket last night. And those jeans were in the laundry basket in the kitchen, ready for the wash! She hurried back into the house.

Funny. She must have left the kitchen light on by mistake. She dashed in and gasped aloud in surprise.

Seated at the kitchen table in their dressing gowns with hair tousled in clumps were Mum and Dad. They looked at her like judges presiding over a very nasty court case. Mum held out a key in her palm.

'Is this perhaps what you're looking for?' she said, in a voice of doom.

'Ah . . . ' Claire said.

'Because we don't think that this is a good time to be going off for a bike ride,' Mum went on, closing her fingers around the key.

'Very bad time for a bike ride,' Dad agreed, frowning at Claire. 'Midnight.'

'*Midnight!*' Mum said, in case Claire hadn't caught it the first time. They were like a double act. Claire wondered vaguely if they'd rehearsed this. She shuffled from one foot to the other awkwardly.

71

'So, what's the explanation for this, young lady?' Mum went on grimly. *Young lady* was a very bad sign.

'Er... I couldn't sleep.'

Dad gave a short theatrical laugh. Not the sort that would have got him very far in a stage career.

'Couldn't sleep? And do you find a quick spin around the block in the middle of the night is helpful?' he said.

There is no lower form of wit than sarcasm, Claire thought, but refrained from saying it. She just shrugged her shoulders.

'It helps.'

'Let's get to the bottom of this, young lady,' Mum took up the running. 'Ben told us this morning that he'd heard you getting up in the middle of last night and going out of the front door. He went through to the spare bedroom and looked out, and saw you cycling off, happy as a butterfly, into the night.'

Claire resolved to strangle Ben in his sleep later on.

'And don't think about any nasty revenge on your brother! He was doing the right thing in telling us about this. In fact he should have woken us up and told us about it there and then, not in the morning. But some misguided sense of loyalty made him go back to bed. He said he was going to wait up until you came back, but he fell asleep waiting.'

That wouldn't save the little beast.

'So. We're waiting for your explanation. Please sit down at the table here with us.'

Mum folded her arms. Reluctantly Claire joined them

at the table. Too close for comfort. What on earth could she say? It had to be plausible.

'It's . . . I just cycle around.'

'Claire! The truth please.'

'I . . . I . . . meet up with someone else.'

Dad looked like a cat who has got the mouse by the tail.

'Ah! Now we're getting to it! And who is this fellow participant in the *Tour de Oxbury*?'

'Just a friend from school.'

'Go on.'

'It's someone . . . it's a new person. New to the school.'

'Go on.'

'An Irish person.' Now she was blushing like a traffic light going to red. Maddening.

'An Irish *person*?' Mum said mercilessly.

'An Irish . . . *boy*?' Dad suggested, in the manner of Sherlock Holmes.

'Yes.'

Both Mum and Dad sat back in their chairs with looks of grim satisfaction. Now they'd got to the bottom of it all right. Young love eh? Raising its ugly head a bit earlier than expected, at thirteen years and one month, but at least it was an explanation.

'Right,' Mum said after a pause. Her voice was a little gentler. 'Let's hear about what you get up to with this Irish boy.'

Claire stumbled through an embarrassing account of moonlit cycling about the streets and long heart to heart

73

conversations under the street lights. That anyone should do anything so pathetic was beyond belief, but her mum and dad seemed to swallow it all. Maybe *their* courting days were spent cycling hither and thither. It wouldn't surprise her. At long last the court was adjourned, and sentencing suspended until the following morning.

Claire trooped miserably up to bed, glancing malevolently towards the open door of her brother's room. Gentle innocent snores came out of there. Let him sleep peacefully while he could, she thought. He would suffer soon enough.

Claire lay for a long time finding it hard to sleep in spite of her tiredness. She drifted in and out of nightmares, in which mysterious shadowy figures came into her room and rode around it in silence. They were dark, hooded figures, wielding scythes. They were perhaps on horseback, but bobbing up and down as if on the kind of horses to be found on a carousel at a fairground. Every time she started out of sleep and opened her eyes, they vanished. But as soon as she closed her eyelids they came back, circling the room in solemn trotting silence.

10
Greengates

'I am going to kill you!' Claire hissed at Ben under cover of the sound of pouring corn flakes.

Ben adopted a hurt look. He layered another half inch slab of margarine onto his toast and licked the knife before putting it back in the tub.

'You should have asked me along, then it would have been all right. I've got a bike as well, you know.'

Claire was about to squash such presumption when Mum came into range.

'Your dad and I want to have another word with you tonight, Claire,' she said. 'In the meantime, just leave Ben alone.'

'I wasn't . . . ' Claire started to protest.

'Yes you were,' her mum interrupted. 'Now just concentrate on getting to school on time!'

At school, Claire was desperate to talk to Aidan. She wanted to know everything. Had he been back to the castle? Had he met up with Dicie again? She felt very agitated.

She shook off her friend Katy at morning break on some pretended errand to the school office, and embarked on a thorough search. But Aidan was nowhere to be seen.

At lunchtime she persuaded Katy that they should try to get more exercise for their figures, and walked her mercilessly around the premises while they chattered away as usual. After about three circuits of the playground, the tuck shop, the hall, and miscellaneous corridors, Katy said, 'Doesn't seem to be here today, does he?'

'What?' Claire said.

'Oh, come on! You're looking for Aidan! All the time we've been walking about your head has been swivelling around like a yo-yo.'

'Yo-yos don't swivel,' Claire responded weakly. 'They go up and down.'

'Don't change the subject.'

'There is no *subject*! I don't know what you're on about!'

'Yeah, right! Well anyway, if you don't mind, could we maybe sit down for a bit in the hall?'

'All right then.'

They made their way to the hall, which was kept open during lunch hour for general milling about in. There were plastic bucket chairs all around the edge, one of the few places you could sit down at break times, since the classrooms were off limits. Bobser and one or two of his unsavoury friends were hovering about, and Bobser waved Claire and Katy towards a chair with a great display of friendly politeness. But even the most cursory glance revealed the blob of fresh chewing gum waiting there for the unwary.

76

'We're not going to sit on your chewing gum, although it's very kind of you to offer,' Katy said, and they made their way to a quiet corner and sat down.

'So, Aidan seems to be away ill or something, doesn't he?' Katy said.

'I suppose he must be.'

'How come you've got friendly with him anyway? When do you see him?'

Claire was almost overcome with the desire to tell Katy all about the Nightland. It was the most exciting and extraordinary thing that had happened in her whole life, and she would have loved to share it with her best friend. But she fought down the impulse. After all, how would she react if Katy announced out of the blue that she went off to another world at night time, travelling by bicycle. She'd be quite certain that it was all just dreams.

She became aware of Katy's face hovering in front of her own, wearing an expression of exaggerated fascination, as if she were a scientist examining an alien life form.

'Well? Why the long pause? It wasn't a very complicated question.'

'Sorry, Katy. I feel so tired, and I just drift off a bit.'

'You do look tired, that's true.'

'Can we not talk about Aidan, just for now? There's no big secret – we just meet up after school occasionally for a talk, on the way home. But I'm a bit worried about him.'

'Why?'

'Just – he doesn't seem very well at the moment.'

'Oh ...'

'Listen – there's nothing more to it. Where did you get that bracelet by the way?'

'Changing the subject!'

'Yes. I am. Where did you get it?'

'Bangles Bazaar, but ...'

'It would go well with that blue dress you've got ...'

Claire managed to turn the conversation around to clothes and shopping, never too difficult with Katy. Then there was a rumpus over on the other side of the hall, where Elizabeth Shove had just sat on Bobser's chewing gum. So the subject of Aidan was successfully dropped.

The afternoon lessons dragged by. Miss Marslop droned on about the eating habits of the brontosaurus while lumbering slowly up and down the aisles of desks like some huge swamp-loving dinosaur herself. Although she tried to pay attention, Claire found her thoughts persistently drifting away to that mysterious world of the night.

Particularly, she kept revolving in her mind the sparse information she had about Dicie. Dicie Ravenscroft. Who went to school at Greengates School on the Banford Road. Who played the harp and claimed that you could stay in the Nightland after moonset. If that was true, and days or even weeks passed in the Nightland while nothing changed here in this world, then presumably Dicie might possibly be found emerging from Greengates School at the end of school today, like any normal schoolgirl. Her extended visit would have been just a momentary absence at midnight.

Claire thought about this. If Aidan wasn't around, it would be comforting to see Dicie, and ask her if she'd seen him. Or, if not comforting, at least...well...something. It was Friday afternoon. The weekend would be torture if she couldn't get any news. They got out at half past three on a Friday. She wondered if Greengates would keep the same hours.

The Banford Road was a long road, but she could reach the near end of it with a ten-minute walk, and make her way along it until she came across the school. She had a mental picture of where the school might be, although she'd never met anyone who went to it. There was a cluster of big rambling Victorian buildings about half way along the road, and it was most likely one of those.

Of course it was pretty hit and miss, whether or not she succeeded in seeing Dicie. It might well be too late by the time she reached the right place. But now she'd got the idea, it had to be pursued. She felt in the grip of an obsession. She had to know what happened last night. Only Miss Marslop's sudden and quite impressive impersonation of a Tyrannosaurus Rex pouncing on its prey recalled her to the present moment.

As the dusk gathered itself ready to spring into full-blown night, Claire was standing in puzzlement outside a pair of big stone gateposts on the Banford Road. There was a slight bend in the road here, and the lights of passing cars swept across the gateposts like spotlights. On the left-hand pillar, the carved offspring of an unfortunate liaison between an eagle and a puffin held in its claws a scroll with some Latin message written on it. On the right-hand post an angry looking ostrich clutched a banner in its beak. On the banner was carved 'Greengates School'.

There were no schoolchildren to be seen. That might have meant that she had simply arrived too late. But there was a blue metallic sign sticking out of a rhododendron bush just inside the gates. The sign said 'compu-dot.com plc'.

That was confusing, and so was the fact that through the big windows of the building, set back amongst Scots pines twenty metres from the road, Claire could see that the brightly-lit rooms within were filled with lots of men and women sitting at computer workstations. Not a school then, by the looks of things.

Just as she was about to turn away, baffled, an oldish lady in a smart business suit strode out of the front door and headed down the driveway towards Claire, swinging her briefcase like a pendulum in one hand, and, in opposite and equal measure, a striped golf umbrella in the other. She looked as if she would run over anything that got in her way, but Claire timidly accosted her as she headed out of the gates.

'Excuse me . . . '

The businesswoman looked at her over the top of half-spectacles.

'Yes?'

'I was looking for Greengates School. Has it moved?'

'Moved?'

Claire pointed at the right-hand gatepost. The business-woman looked at it and smiled.

'Ah – I see. Greengates School. No, it hasn't moved, dear. But I *do* happen to know all about it.'

She paused, to lend a little drama to the mystery.

'It closed down, dear, during the War.' She looked harder at Claire, who had no suitable facial expression with which to receive this news. 'The Second World War, you know. All the children were evacuated...' This she illustrated by indicating two points on the ground with the tip of her umbrella. '...and the headmistress, who owned the school, was nearing retirement age. So she sold up and went to live in Cornwall. Polperro. A nice little cottage by the harbour, with a view of the sea. She had a half-tame seagull called Sammy the Seagull. And how would I know all this, do you think?'

Claire just gaped at her.

'Well...' Here the golf umbrella was flourished like a magic wand. '...the headmistress was my grand-mother! There! And now, by sheer fluke and coincidence, I work in the room that used to be her study! Programming. I'm the oldest computer program-mer on earth. Or at least it sometimes seems like that to me. Well, good day to you!'

And the lady marched off again like a brisk mechanical toy, arms swinging.

Claire made her way home – about a half hour's walk – in the midst of a mental fog. She found her way automatically, for her thoughts were all far off, in Nightland. Had Dicie really said *Greengates* or had she misheard her? Or had Dicie made some dreadful miscalculation, and by staying in Nightland too long, missed her chance to return to her own world at the right time? And what about Aidan? Where was *he* right now?

By the time she got home, Claire felt more confused than she'd ever been in her life, and couldn't even be bothered to fight Ben for the television remote control. She sat on the sofa in a dream, wondering what on earth she was going to do.

11
In the Churchyard

It was Saturday morning and the weekend stretched out before Claire like a desert without an oasis. Why hadn't she and Aidan exchanged telephone numbers? She knew he lived somewhere in Archersfield, but that was a great maze of neat little terraced houses built in red brick, most of which sported a hanging basket of flowers dangling under a tiny covered porch. Her father called it Toytown, and when Aidan said that's where he lived she told him the name. He'd laughed and said that must explain why his neighbour had such big ears. 'Big Ears... Noddy... get it?' he'd explained, and she'd groaned.

The phone book held no clue. There were no McCaffreys at all in Oxbury according to that. If she'd thought about it at the end of school on Friday she might have got the phone number from Mrs Sawdon in the school office with some story about borrowing a book or something, but now the office would be closed until Monday morning.

Ben wanted to go for a bike ride. Dad, who occasionally went for rides with him, had to go to work that morning. Mum, who never willingly bestrode a bicycle, pleaded preparations for a dinner party that evening. Ben wasn't considered old and sensible enough to cycle very far on his own. That left Claire.

'Go *on*, Claire!' he pleaded. '*You* go off cycling enough!'

That wasn't a very tactful thing to say, in view of his treachery.

'Why should I do you any favours?' Claire said huffily.

Ben glanced over his shoulder. No adults in earshot.

'Well . . . supposing, just supposing, you were to want to go off cycling one night. And, just supposing I happened to wake up and hear you going . . . well, perhaps I might not wake up properly . . . perhaps I might not wake up enough to tell Mum and Dad what you were doing?'

Claire eyed him severely. 'You little briber!'

'Take it or leave it!'

Claire thought about it. She might well want to sneak off again in the night. In fact, the thought of not seeing the Nightland again was too hard to bear. It was unimaginable. In fact . . . perhaps she could go there on her own, without Aidan. Tonight. Perhaps she'd meet him there. A thrill of excitement went through her. But she kept her face calm, and nodded at Ben with apparent reluctance.

'All right then, beast! As a *special* favour to you. Let's get ready.'

It was a bright wintry day. The sun was low in the sky, and the trees, buildings, people, and even the cats and dogs of Oxbury cast long skinny shadows on the ground beneath them. Up above, birds on the wing glinted like little silver spacecraft darting by. It was the kind of day that sank into your heart and made you feel good. Claire felt refreshed and happy as she and Ben cycled towards the park with the cold air rushing into their faces. Sunshine! Even winter sunshine – what could be better?

At the park, Ben did wheelies on the bumpy ground near the duck pond. Claire looked at the ducks squabbling for bread thrown by toddlers and their parents. There was a long dark reflection in the water, and she raised her eyes and saw the steeple of St Mary's of Oxbury pointing like a thin finger at the sky. It was right beside the park, and there was a gate in the low stone wall between the park and the churchyard. On an impulse, Claire called out to Ben.

'I'm just going up the slope there to the churchyard! I can still see you over the wall! Don't go off anywhere!'

'Okay!' came Ben's response. He was the intrepid motor cycle scrambler Daredevil Dan. He needed to work up to a new speed record over the famous Duck Pond Hills course. Especially before any park keeper came up and reminded him that cycling was not allowed on the grass!

Claire wasn't sure Ben had really heard what she'd said, but she wasn't going far away. Personally she thought that Ben was old enough to cycle on his own in the park anyway, and didn't need the services of a guardian older sister.

She leaned her bike against the churchyard wall, and

padlocked it, just in case. She liked the churchyard. She and Ben used to play hide-and-seek amongst the gravestones when they were little. Mum used to keep a lookout, guiltily, for the vicar. Maybe she'd get Ben up here for a quick game of hide-and-seek in a minute.

She wandered along, reading the inscriptions on the graves. She already knew some of them by heart. There was her namesake Claire Swift in here somewhere. She'd got a fright when she was little, when Mum had pointed out that gravestone to her. She'd thought it had been put there in readiness for her. But in fact Claire Swift had died in 1930, the dearly beloved wife of Oswald Swift. They'd both lived to ninety. They weren't relations of their own, as far as Mum and Dad knew. There were little family groups of graves though, where you could trace two hundred years or more in the generations, the same Christian names cropping up over and over again. There were stones for people with the same names as her friends at school, or her teachers. Was Martin Marslop (died 1921), for example, the grandfather of Miss Marslop the biology teacher? And was the little line of Smyths anything to do with Jenny and Robert Smyth in Years Eight and Nine?

And here was another familiar name, Ravenscroft. *Ravenscroft*. For a moment, Claire couldn't think why it was familiar. Then it rushed back into her memory. Of course. Dicie *Ravenscroft*. She scrutinised the inscription. 'Albert Ravenscroft 1889–1918. Beloved husband of Agnes. Died in action, serving his country.

86

Agnes Ravenscroft 1890–1965. May they rest in peace.'

There was another gravestone next to this one. A small one, leaning at a slight angle. Ivy had twined itself around it, but not obscured the inscription. 'Eurydice Ravenscroft' it said. '1910–1923. Beloved daughter of Agnes and Albert. Taken from this Vale of Tears to a happier, better place.'

Claire stood as still as the stone angel on the war memorial behind her. Eurydice Ravenscroft. *Dicie* Ravenscroft, who'd said she went to Greengates School – a school that had closed down more than fifty years ago. Was *this* the thirteen-year-old girl she had met in the Nightland only two nights ago?

The gravestones, the church steeple, the low winter sun, the trees in the park beyond the wall – everything spun around her head as if some supernatural power was juggling with the world. She stood transfixed, dizzy, about to topple over with her thoughts and fears. A voice spoke at her elbow.

'*Here* you are! Do you want to play hide-and-seek?'

She turned her head slowly, as if it might fall off. Ben was standing beside her, looking so happy and hopeful and full of life that she felt like hugging him. Luckily he ran off to hide before she could translate this confusing emotion into action.

12
What Happened to Aidan?

That afternoon Claire told Mum she was going to call on her friend Katy. Then she set off towards Toytown. She had no idea how she might locate Aidan's home, but she couldn't just sit around the house with her new knowledge. She was filled with a restless agitation that would be unbearable unless she was actually doing something, however futile.

Toytown was enjoying the winter sunshine. Serious-looking men were lathering soap suds over their shiny cars and buffing the bonnets until they could see their reflections. Small children muffled up in great quilted jackets were often nearby, carrying sloshing buckets of water or pedalling furiously up and down on their three-wheelers. Dog owners stepped briskly along the pavements, or stopped and pretended to be intrigued by something on the other side of the road while their pet befouled someone else's gateway. In short, it was a scene of suburban bliss.

How did one find a missing McCaffrey amongst all of this? It was like looking for a button in a beanbag. But, for the second time that day, the mysterious foot of coincidence stepped in.

Claire had been wandering up and down for half an

hour or more when, rounding a corner, she almost bumped into two weary-looking men in postman's uniforms. They were pulling little trolleys behind them, like the shopping bags on wheels favoured by some old ladies. Presumably they had just made a late end to the Saturday morning deliveries.

Claire stood aside for them, and then had a brainwave.

'Er – excuse me!' she said.

'Yes?' replied the older of the two men, a white-bearded fellow who would have looked at home on the bridge of a ship.

'I wondered if you could help me. I was looking for Mr and Mrs McCaffrey's house.'

'McCaffrey. Twenty-eight Longbow Lane. Used to be the Calders,' replied the ancient mariner without hesitation. The younger postman shook his head, whether in admiration or pity Claire couldn't tell.

'Thank you! Thank you very much! Longbow Lane is . . . '

'The same way as you're going. First turning on the left.'

'Thank you!'

The house was the same as all the others, neat and tidy. At this time of year there were no flowers in the hanging basket in the porch, but it was there, in readiness.

Claire knocked timidly at the door. A white door, freshly painted. There was quite a long pause, and she was about to knock again when she heard footsteps within, and a man of about forty opened the door and looked enquiringly at her.

She was sure immediately that this was Aidan's father. He had the same shaped face, and kindly eyes. But he looked a little unwell, or perhaps just tired.

'Hello, I'm a friend of Aidan's from school. This is Aidan McCaffrey's house, is it?'

'Yes. And what's your name, my dear?' The man's voice was low, but his Irish accent was unmistakable.

'Claire. Claire Swift.'

'Pleased to meet you. Aidan hasn't told me about you, but then he wouldn't tell his old dad about his girl-friends, now would he?'

Claire smiled, a little embarrassed.

'Is Aidan at home?' she asked.

An expression that Claire couldn't understand crossed the man's face like a cloud.

'Oh . . . you haven't heard of course.'

'Sorry? Heard what?'

Mr McCaffrey put his hand to his forehead and massaged his temple. He took a deep breath before replying.

'Something very strange has happened. On Friday morning we couldn't find Aidan. He wasn't in bed or anywhere about the house. We didn't know what could have happened to him. After talking about it, we thought it best to tell the police. They told us that a boy had just been found on a road outside town – Crows Wood Lane. It sounded like Aidan. He was in a coma. Not injured, as far as could be seen, but in a coma.'

Mr McCaffrey's eyes met Claire's. She could read all the anxiety and perplexity in his mind.

'We went to Southlands Hospital. It *was* Aidan. His mother's with him there now, and I'm just going back in a little while.'

Claire's heart was thumping.

'In hospital? Then, what ... ?'

'He's just lying there, as if in a deep sleep. The doctors don't know why.'

Night fell on Oxbury like a dark cloak. But the Swift household was a blaze of lights as Claire and Ben's mum and dad prepared to entertain their friends the Holwills, the Tulletts and the MacGregors.

On these occasions Dad was cast in the role of Igor, lumbering brutish servant to the brilliant Mrs Frankenstein who masterminded the whole affair.

'No, no, no, Mike! *Not* on the mantelpiece. On the main table! What's the point of putting the candle holder the Holwills gave us where they won't even see it?'

'Sorry,' Dad muttered, and moved the candle holder. Claire wasn't certain how much Dad enjoyed entertaining. Or at least the preparations for it. Once the wine was on the go he was transformed. The house rang with his repeated 'ho! ho! ho!', for all the world as if a demented Father Christmas had got in through the chimney. The sound carried all the way up the stairs, and kept you awake.

However, Claire was not intending to sleep that night.

91

Once the adults had eaten their supper, they'd all go and lounge about in the sitting room and see who could make the most noise. It would be child's play to sneak out under cover of the racket.

She had spent the afternoon and evening turning the situation around and around in her head. If Aidan was in hospital, in a coma, then did that mean he had come back from the Nightland? Or was he still there, somehow? Was some part of him taken – his spirit, or his soul – while his physical body was lying on a hospital bed? Had he gone back to the castle on Thursday night, when she had been prevented from joining him? And had Dicie, the long-dead Dicie Ravenscroft, persuaded him to stay until the moon set in Nightland, and the Reapers emerged from the shadows?

It was a long and weary wait for the bustle downstairs to move from the dining table in the kitchen to the sitting room. But at last Claire heard the noisy troupe on the move up the stairs and into their new habitat.

'Ho! Ho! Ho!' she heard her dad roaring, and there was an accompanying giggling noise, like birds twittering. Then the living-room door was shut and the noise was slightly muffled, as if the party were carrying on under a layer of pillows.

She crept out of the house, trying not to think of the awful consequences if Mum or Dad took it into their heads to climb up to her bedroom later on. When she and Ben were little, Mum once told her, they would always take a last doting look at their sleeping infants before turning in themselves. However, this was apparently no longer a part of the parental routine.

The night was very cold, the black sky sprinkled with stars. The moon was nowhere to be seen. Claire cycled purposefully towards Crows Wood Lane, and then turned along it, beyond the reach of the street lights. The darkness held no terrors for her. She was entirely focused on her objective. She pedalled harder and harder, heedless of the danger of crashing, as she knew she had to be if she was to break through the mysterious barrier and reach the Nightland.

At last she found herself on that steep slope down to the river. The bridge was before her. As her bike flew over the hump and landed on the far side, she heard a voice behind her.

'Cl...aaai......re..............!' came a long trailing cry. She braked quickly and looked back in bewilderment. Hurtling towards her across the bridge was a small bullet-like figure with a terrified face. It skidded to a breathless halt beside her. Her brother Ben stared at her with a look of admiration.

13
A Rescue Mission

'Wow! Claire! I never thought a girl could ride like that! Coming down that hill was the fastest I've ever gone!'

'Why did you follow me?' Claire said coldly.

'I couldn't sleep with the noise from downstairs. And I thought it might be fun to come with you. You're not going to be grumpy and spoil it, are you?'

Claire felt inclined to be grumpy. She'd got a long and perhaps dangerous mission ahead of her, and she didn't need a sidekick.

'Well, now you've had your fun, why don't you just cycle back across that bridge and home again?'

Ben gave her his wounded hamster impression, complete with small mewling noise.

'Stop it!'

Ben went into hamster about to expire from cruel treatment mode.

'Stop it! This isn't a joke. Your cute tricks aren't going to work this time.'

Ben switched off the hamster and went straight to plan B.

'All right. I'll go back. And I'll go in to Mum and Dad and tell them where I left you. 'Bye!'

Claire looked at Ben as if he were a piece of chewing

94

gum that had got stuck to her shoe. It looked as if she wouldn't be able to prise him off. She sighed.

'All right. You can stay with me. But only as long as you do exactly what I say, all right?'

'Brilliant. How come it's suddenly quite warm by the way?'

'Well . . . ' Claire was wondering how to start explaining things, but now Ben was looking upwards at the sky.

'There wasn't a moon a few minutes ago.'

'We've crossed over into another place. It's all different here. It's called the Nightland.'

Ben was looking at her as if she was babbling.

'Crossing the bridge – it's something to do with crossing the bridge,' she went on, waving a hand towards it. 'I don't really understand it either. Come on, just cycle up this slope in front of us, and you'll see.'

They laboured up the hill, Ben breathlessly firing questions at Claire.

But when they got to the top he fell silent as the magical view of forests and mountains bathed in silver moonlight spread out below them.

'Wow! Where are we? This place looks amazing!'

'I told you, it's called the Nightland.'

'Who calls it that?'

'What do you mean, who?'

'Well – who?'

'Aidan told me it was called that.'

'Aidan? That Irish kid at school?'

'Yes.'

'What's he got to do with it?'

'He brought me here first. He showed me how to get here.'

'Wow! Is he an alien or something?'

'*What?*'

'An alien. Or something.'

'Don't be ridiculous. You only get aliens in films and books.'

Ben gestured to the landscape in front of them.

'You might have said you only got places like this in films and books.'

'Well this is different.'

'It certainly is.'

Claire had a sudden surge of impatience with her younger brother. She remembered the urgency of her mission and the possible danger that lay ahead.

'Listen, Ben. I don't have time to argue about aliens and things. I'd much prefer it if you just cycled back over that bridge.'

'No way, Jose! This place looks great!'

'Well, I'm only taking you with me if you *promise* to do as I say. We've got to go a long way, and we can't waste time.'

'You're the boss.'

'Yes. Just remember that and we'll be all right.'

'But...'

'Come on...' Claire pushed away down the hill. She'd got a slice of fruit cake in her jeans pocket for the three-headed dog, which she could hear faintly barking in the woods below.

'But what are we doing?' Ben said, as he drew level with her.

Claire told Ben all about the Nightland as they cycled down the long track lined with yew trees. About the dog, the reapers, the village, the courtroom, the river and the ferryman, the castle. About Donny and Jake, and their lost brother, and Aidan, and Dicie Ravenscroft. About her fears for Aidan, lying in a coma in hospital. He asked an occasional stupid question, but on the whole she was pleased with his ready understanding and acceptance of what she told him. He drew comparisons with stories he'd read or films he'd seen, and had even come across a three-headed dog before, in some story from ancient Greece told to his class by their history teacher.

That didn't completely prepare him for the sight of the real thing however. As the creature came bounding towards them, all three heads barking furiously, he skidded to a halt behind Claire.

'It's all right. Look, he likes cake.'

Claire broke the slice of fruit cake into three segments and threw them in different directions. Each of the heads spotted a different one, and tried to make for it. For several seconds the poor beast lurched from one side to another, without getting any nearer to any of the cake.

'Come on!' Claire said to Ben, who looked petrified. 'This is our chance to get past him!'

They sped through the yew tree gate and out into the

fields of corn where the ghostly reapers laboured over their endless task. There was a faint wind rippling through the corn, a warm wind. It made the stalks rustle and whisper, like a great crowd of people. They gained the forest on the further side of the fields, and began cycling through the silent ranks of pine trees, the moon sailing high above them like a ghostly lantern.

Suddenly, emerging from the dark trees into a moonlit glade, Claire saw something hurtling towards her with terrible speed! She braked hard and yelled, 'Look out!'

It was a cyclist, head down, going at a reckless pace. The cyclist's head lifted at the sound of Claire's cry, and just in time he slewed off the path and was pitched off his bike into the soft hummocky grass. A second cyclist came flying into the glade and skidded to a halt. Ben came shooting past Claire, jammed on his brakes, and flew over his handlebars to land in a heap beside the other fallen figure.

'Struth! You frightened the life out of us, Claire!' Donny said, sitting up in the grass next to his bike. Its front wheel was up in the air, spinning gently to a halt.

'Are you all right, Ben?' Claire said, dismounting.

Ben nodded. He was too winded to speak.

Jake helped Donny to get up, while Claire dusted Ben off.

'Where were you going in such a hurry?' Claire said.

'We might ask the same thing,' Donny said, rubbing his knee. 'You were going like a storm there!'

'So where were you going?' she repeated.

'To Australia.'

'That's this way, is it?'

'Yeah. Eventually.'

'That's funny, because we were coming from England along this way.'

'Funny place this, altogether. Anyway, we're not coming back.'

'What! Why not?'

Donny joined in. 'We found Mikey!'

'Your older brother? Fantastic! That's what you wanted, isn't it, all this time?'

'Yeah. We found him down by the river, beyond the courthouse.'

'Waiting to cross? Near the ferryman?'

'Yeah.'

'And he could see you?'

'Yeah. He came out of the crowd to talk to us. We probably wouldn't have spotted him otherwise. He was wearing these kind of white robe things. Not what he'd wear at home.'

'So, what did he say? Is he ... dead?'

'Seems it's not as straightforward as that. Can't say I really understood it properly. Said he was going to go down to the ocean.'

'What, beyond the castle?'

'Yeah. Long way away. Said he'd been thinking about it a long time, and now he was going.'

'But what's so significant about that?'

Jake took up the story.

'You're missing stuff out, Donny. Claire – Mikey told us stuff about the Nightland that we didn't know. You come here when you're dead all right, but you can also come in here while you're alive...'

'We know that,' Donny interrupted. 'We've been doing that for ages.'

'Let me explain,' Jake said. 'Just butt out for a minute. It's not so simple. Apparently you can hang out here indefinitely. You're kind of allocated to somewhere by the judges in the courthouse. Where you go depends on the kind of life you've led.'

'What – whether you've been good or wicked? Like heaven and hell?' Claire said.

'Not exactly as simple as that apparently. Mikey got to go to some place that wasn't so very different from the ranch back home, so it was kind of neutral, except that he missed us and Mum and Dad. Some people get sent to less pleasant places. But wherever you end up, you've got the choice of staying there, or moving on.'

'Moving on?' Claire said.

'Yeah. You can go down to the ocean and get on some kind of ship. Mikey wasn't too sure of the details, because once you do that, once you set off on this ship, you can never come back.'

Claire remembered the tapestries in the castle. The skeletons on the ship in the harbour, and the living figures of flesh and blood on the ship out at sea.

'So no one knows what happens after that,' Donny explained.

'So, how did Mikey decide whether to stay or go?' Claire asked.

'That's the difficulty, apparently,' Donny replied. 'Most of the people here just stay put. Most of them are scared to move on. Mikey says there's all kinds of rumours about what happens after you get onto that ocean. Some say you go back to the real world and live all over again. Others say you go to heaven or hell. Others say there's another shore on the far side, and it's just another place like this, that you just keep going around in circles.'

Claire tried to grasp this.

'So . . . this place, the Nightland, it isn't the end?'

'It *can* be. Or you can carry on. That's what Mikey's decided to do. Then you get kitted out in these white robes and head off to the ocean to get your ship.'

Ben piped up.

'I thought when you died you'd just kind of fall asleep, and that would be that. Just darkness forever. Nothing.'

'This is my brother Ben,' Claire said.

'Pleased to meet you, Ben,' Jake said.

'Good on you, mate!' Donny added. 'Well, you may be right. Maybe all of this is a kind of dream that happens when you're dead.'

Ben looked worried.

'No, I don't mean you're dead now! But it's a dangerous place this. Mikey said we shouldn't be taking our chances, coming in here. He said it wasn't worth it. He got caught in here, and that was that. He's lost the whole mortal life he could have had.'

101

'That's why we're here,' Claire said. She was getting onto her bike now as the urgency of her mission returned to her. 'We've got to get moving again. Aidan's here – I think, at the castle.'

'Aidan? You mean he didn't go back?' Jake asked.

'He's in a coma. In the real world. He might die.'

'Struth! And you want to get him back?' Donny said.

'Yes.'

'Too late. Forget it.'

'I can't. I won't. He's not dead yet.'

'You can't leave, once you've stayed after the moonset.'

'Do you *know* that?'

'Mikey said so. The Reapers...'

Claire didn't want to hear any more. She turned to Ben.

'Come on, Ben! It's time we got moving.'

'But...'

'COME ON! Remember what I said. I'm the boss, right?'

Ben straddled his bicycle again.

'Well, good luck to you, Claire!' Donny said. 'Make sure you're out by moonset, that's all!'

'Yeah, good luck. Don't take any chances. You've got your whole lives ahead of you,' Jake added. 'That's why we're going to stay out of this for good. We'll end up here in the end anyway.'

''Bye! Good luck! Maybe I'll come and see you in Australia one day!' Claire said. Then she and Ben pushed on their pedals and resumed their journey, cycling even faster to make up for lost time.

14
The King of the Castle

Eventually Claire and Ben came out of the trees near the back of the courthouse. They descended through the lush green meadows to the river, where the grumpy old ferryman was working away as usual, ferrying droves of silent wraiths across the turbulent water. This was Ben's first close-up sight of the wraiths, and he stared at them nervously.

'So, are these all dead people, Claire?'

'As far as I know, yes.'

'And you're sure they can't see us?'

'They don't pay any attention to us, even if they can. Come on, don't be scared now, or you'll have to go back on your own.'

Ben looked as if he thought this was the scariest option of all.

They made their way to the jetty, wheeling their bikes. The ferryman fixed his red eyes on Claire.

'You again eh? Going back to the castle eh?'

'Yes.'

'But you've brought a different boy this time I see.'

'My brother.'

'Ah...and bicycles again, I see. How shall you pay for your passage?'

His red eyes glowed greedily, and he gave a great thump to one of the wraiths who was edging towards the empty boat.

'Back you! Wait your turn!'

Turning back to Claire and Ben he jerked his head towards the crowd of wraiths.

'They're so impatient. They'll spend the rest of eternity on the other side of this river, but they still can't wait to cross over.'

'Can't they come back?' Ben said. Claire detected a note of fear in his voice.

The ferryman turned his terrible red eyes on Ben.

'No, young whippersnapper mortal. They can *never* come back across the waters of the river of lamentation.'

He stared with such frightening intensity as he spoke these gloomy words, that Ben took half a step backwards.

'Have you the payment for your crossing, young mortals? Not forgetting the extra trouble of the bicycles?'

This time Claire had come prepared. She offered the ferryman two pound coins. He took them eagerly, sniffed them, bit them with his yellow stumpy teeth, and slipped them into the small bag that lay in his boat. As an afterthought, he took out the little dark bottle that he kept in the bag, and took a deep swig from it.

'That's better. Now, hop aboard and look alive, before I change my mind. You do know that I'm breaking the rules for you, I suppose? You're not supposed to come across here unless you've been buried. Properly buried as well, with all the ceremonies.'

Grumbling, he ferried them across the bubbling river, and without regrets they disembarked and cycled off quickly.

'What a horrible old man!' Ben said. 'I don't know why, but something about him reminds me of something I learned at school.'

'What do you mean?'

'I don't know. There was some story about a ferryman and a river.'

They cycled on, Claire setting as fast a pace as she could. At last the great castle reared up ahead of them, its pennants fluttering in the white moon wind, its towering walls rising like cliffs into the sky. The gates were thronging with people, great silent droves of wraiths milling about. In the courtyard beyond the gates, there were hundreds of horses tethered to railings around the walls. Bored-looking soldier wraiths were guarding them, or feeding them hay.

'There must be a lot of visitors,' Claire said thoughtfully. 'Perhaps something special is going on.'

She turned to Ben. 'I want you to wait here, by the gate, with the bicycles.'

'Oh...Claire...'

'You *promised* to do as I told you!'

Ben struggled with the instincts of a lifetime. It didn't come easily to do what his sister told him. But he *had* promised that she would be the boss.

'Okay.'

They looked about for somewhere to put the bikes. There was a kind of recess in the wall right under the arch of the gate. It might have been intended as a place for guards to stand, but it was empty. They pushed their bikes into this alcove and Claire gave a sudden exclamation.

'Look!'

There was another bicycle already in there. She looked at it carefully.

It was a boy's bike, and it had a water bottle on it.

'I'm sure this is Aidan's bike!' she said to Ben. 'Now – stay exactly here. Don't go wandering off. We might want to leave in a hurry.'

She glanced back through the gate. The moon was still high. But she remembered how quickly it could set. There was no time to be lost.

Claire made her way alone through the silent crowd. She looked at the faces of the wraiths, to see if there was any clue to what they were doing here. Were they happy or sad? Frightened or bold? She couldn't tell. They had the expressions of sleepwalkers, and although they moved hither and thither ceaselessly, there was no indication that they were coming from anywhere in particular, or going to anywhere definite.

She hurried up the steps and into the castle. Standing at the end of the long torchlit corridor hung with tapestries, she could immediately hear the sound of revelry up ahead. There was a busy droning buzz of voices, like a beehive, interspersed with clinkings and clatterings and clunkings, as if knives were scraping plates, and goblets being clashed together in toasts. Occasionally there was a great roar of laughter.

There were guards with halberds stationed at the entrance to the banqueting hall, but Claire walked boldly past them and pushed open the great wooden door. They didn't appear to notice.

Inside, the banqueting hall was filled to the brim with feasting wraiths. There were great fat guzzling lords with tankards of wine the size of small buckets at their elbows. They dabbled their greasy fingers deep in the remains of chickens, turkeys and swans. There were dainty ladies in flowing muslin veils and tall pointed head-pieces, feeding morsels to a scurrying pack of small dogs. There was also a tiny piglet, which ran excitedly from one source of food to another. There was a jester in bells and clothes made from multicoloured patches of cloth, who was walking on his hands along the tables, causing screams of hilarity as he threatened to overbalance onto this or that person's plate of food. Hundreds of torches and candles lit the scene with a capricious uncertain light, as if countless yellow and orange glow-worms were creeping about.

At the high table sat the king and queen of the castle. The king was a huge figure, even seated, and his golden crown caught the flickering light and reflected it, so that as he moved his head this way or that, he appeared to be crowned with flames. He had a great black beard, and

107

his dark eyes were sunk deep in his head. For all the merriment around him, Claire thought he looked cold and forbidding.

His queen sat on his right-hand side. She was as pale as the king was dark. She was the most transparent wraith Claire had ever seen in the Nightland, no more than a wisp of misty beauty. Her crown was silver, capturing the light of the candles and torches like so many stars and moons glinting in a miniature universe. Her face was timeless, not old or young, and her big eyes were the palest blue that could possibly exist.

To the left of the king sat Dicie. She, like the queen, was a silvery foil to his golden robes and crown. Her long hair was braided, and she wore a gown of cream sewn with glittering tiny green jewels. She was staring straight at Claire, and suddenly clutched the arm of her companion on the opposite side of her to the king. It was Aidan!

15
Music from Heaven

Claire couldn't make out whether Aidan was glad to see her or not. He stared at her as if he'd seen a ghost, and Dicie whispered urgently into his ear. He started to stand up, but she tugged on his sleeve and he sat back down again with a bump. Claire was about to set off around the edge of the frantic scene to reach where they were, when suddenly the king stood up and clapped his hands three times loudly. The 'crack, crack, crack' of his huge palms echoed around the hall like three pistol shots, and the jester sprang high into the air off the end of a table and disappeared into a dark doorway to a ripple of laughter and applause.

The king motioned with a hand, and two servants hurried into the centre of the hall bearing a harp. Stealing occasional glances in her direction, Aidan now stood up, bowed low to the king and queen, and made his way to the harp. A third servant brought in a stool for him to sit on. A hush fell in the great hall, and the queen laid her hand on the king's arm with a smile as they settled in readiness for the music. Aidan was facing away from Claire now, towards the high table. He was exactly half way between Dicie and Claire, and Claire could feel Dicie's eyes burning into her as Aidan ran his fingers across the strings a few times in readiness for playing.

Why could everyone see Aidan, but not see her? Was he already dead, out in the real world? Like Dicie?

Aidan began to play. As if a beautiful colourful bird had glided into the great hall from the moonlit land outside, the stream of notes flowed gracefully through the smoky torchlit air. Claire was spellbound, like everyone else in the place. She felt as if all her fears and worries could wait until the music had ended, that time would stand still for as long as those notes cascaded through the enchanted air. It was a kind of rapture, that robbed her of all will to do anything but stand and listen. For ever, if need be.

There was no way of knowing how long that music played. When it ended, it was as if a dream had faded from the memory, leaving only a lingering sense of joy and peace. The king stood, and the queen got to her feet also, and, in the deep silence that the harp's notes had left behind, there was no sound but the rustle of their robes. Claire thought they would begin to clap, but instead they did something quite extraordinary. Hand in hand, they bowed deeply towards Aidan. Then Aidan stood, and bowed in return. Only then did the king raise his hands to the rest of the hall, so that everyone stood up. When they had done so, he led the applause with great thunderous hand claps whose echoes bounced like cannonballs from the stony vaulted ceiling.

As the servants took away the harp and stool, Claire boldly walked up to Aidan.

'Aidan! What are you doing here? You've got to come back with me!'

Aidan turned wonderingly.

'Claire! I thought it was you there by the door. But you're so faint!'

'What?'

'You're not solid. You're like one of the wraiths.'

'I'm not a wraith. I'm alive and I've come to get you back to the real world – to Oxbury, to your parents.'

'There's no rush, Claire. Time stands still in here. I can come back any time and there'll be no difference.'

'No. It's not like that. Back in Oxbury you're . . .'

But Claire had no time to complete her warning. Dicie had arrived, eyes flashing angrily.

'You shouldn't be here!' she said to Claire.

'Why not?' Claire said.

'Because this is only a place for those who *stay* in the Nightland. It's not a place for visitors.'

'Aidan is only a visitor.'

'No he's not. He's staying here. He's like me. He prefers it here.'

Aidan looked apologetically at Claire. 'We can stay as long as we like. There's no danger. All those stories about Reapers and the darkness . . .'

Claire glanced around her. The tables were full of chattering gaiety again, and nobody seemed to be watching them.

'Listen, Aidan!' she said urgently. 'I don't understand why it is, but back in the real world you're in a coma. In hospital. You might die. Unless you come with me now, you'll never see your parents again.'

'In a coma?' Aidan said. 'But...I'm here. My body is here.'

'No, your body is in a hospital bed, and your mum and dad are petrified.'

'She's making it up!' Dicie said scornfully. 'She just wants to spoil everything.'

'No I don't, Dicie Ravenscroft. How long ago did your father Albert die?'

Dicie looked perplexed. 'How do you know my father's name?'

'Never mind. He died, didn't he? How long ago?'

'Five years ago, when I was eight.'

'And that was in the war, wasn't it?'

'Yes. In France.'

'In 1918?'

'Yes.'

Claire turned to Aidan, who was looking in confusion from her to Dicie and back again.

'You see! Obviously you two don't spend any time talking about the *real* world, or you'd have worked this out by now.'

'Worked *what* out?' Dicie said angrily.

'Worked out that you *died* in the real world in 1923, when you came in here and didn't return.'

112

Dicie laughed. 'How can I have died? Look at me! I'm thirteen.'

'And what year is it, outside in the real world?'

'1923 of course!'

Aidan shook his head. A mixture of pity and horror was written on his face.

'Dicie . . . ' he said gently.

'What?'

'Dicie . . . it's not 1923 any more.'

'What? Well, what is it then?'

'It's 2002.'

Dicie shook her head. 'That's ridiculous. That would mean I'd been here for most of a century. I'd be more than ninety years old.'

Claire felt sorry for her now. Her words were confident and dismissive, but there was something else in her eyes. A kind of fear. Claire couldn't bear to tell her what she knew – that she'd seen her grave in the churchyard at St Mary's of Oxbury. Dicie had to stay in the Nightland now, forever. She was happy here. It was too late to help her anyway. But what about Aidan? Surely it wasn't too late for him . . .

Suddenly they were all aware of a huge shape towering over them. It was the king of the Nightland!

His eyes were like black pits filled with shimmering oil. Reflected in their surfaces were tiny flames. To her surprise and terror, it was obvious that he could see Claire perfectly well. His voice seemed to come from deep underground, like the voice of a volcano getting ready to erupt.

'You do not belong here, girl!' he said. 'Your time has not come. Go back before the moon sets. Go back with your brother, who stands at the gate to my castle, before it is too late.'

Claire trembled, but faced the looming figure as bravely as she could. 'Aidan is coming too. He shouldn't stay here either.'

The king looked towards Aidan. 'Aidan. You bring the music of the heavens to this place. You will be honoured here. I ask you to stay!'

'*Ask?*'

'I have no power to make you stay. You have not yet died in the land of the living. But I tell you now, that if the darkness of the moonset finds you still in my kingdom, then my Reapers will bring you back to me, and you will stay with me forever. You will play your music of the heavens here in the underworld until time itself has come to an end.'

'The underworld? But everyone calls this the Nightland!'

The king threw back his head and laughed. 'What does it matter what you call my kingdom! It has been given many names by mankind. And so have I.'

Dicie was staring at the king.

'How long have I been here?' she said.

'Time does not exist here,' the king replied. 'Your question is meaningless.'

Dicie looked at Aidan. 'Are you going back?'

Aidan nodded. 'I have to.'

'Then I'm coming too.'

'But...' Claire started to object.

'Don't try to stop me!' Dicie said angrily. 'It's all your fault that Aidan has to go back. He was happy here, the same as me. Now you come and spoil it all. Well, I'm coming back too.'

But the king put a hand on her shoulder. 'You cannot go back with these others. Your time has passed, Eurydice. Stay, and be a princess of the Nightland.'

Dicie looked up at him, her eyes beginning to fill with tears. Then she ran quickly out of the hall, sobbing.

The king turned to Aidan. 'You must make your decision swiftly, musician. The moon sails quickly through the sky. I would be glad to have you as my court harpist forever.'

Then he turned away and walked back towards his queen, who was watching solemnly from her seat.

'Come on, Aidan!' Claire pulled urgently at his sleeve. 'My brother Ben is outside, and we've found your bike. We've got to go right now! There's no time to lose.'

Aidan looked around him. 'It's like a dream come true, this world. I...I almost feel I'd rather stay here...'

Claire took his hand and pulled him towards the door. 'Just don't look back, Aidan, all right? Don't look behind you. We've got to get away.'

16
A Problem with the Ferryman

Ben was waiting by the gate.

'You got him!' he exclaimed. 'Hi, Aidan, I'm Ben.'

'Hello,' Aidan said. He still seemed in a daze.

Claire looked up at the sky and a shiver went through her. The moon had moved much lower.

'Come on, let's get going!' she said anxiously.

The three of them set out together along the long road away from the castle. They all pedalled hard, and there was no time for talking. The moon lay straight ahead of them, suspended like a great weight which the sky could no longer support, sinking slowly but inexorably lower towards the horizon. Claire felt as if the nightmare ride would never end. The road went on and on, and the moon went down and down.

Finally they reached the rickety jetty where the ferryman leaned against his oar, as if waiting for them.

'Can you take us back?' Claire said, dismounting. 'I've got more money for you!'

But the old man shook his head, and a grim smile twisted his lips.

'What? We'll pay you, I said!'

'Orders have been received. I dare not let you cross.'

'Orders from who? What are you talking about?'

116

'The king. He likes his music, does the king. Between you and me, I don't think he wants to lose his musician.'

The old man's red eyes rested on Aidan, and he set his long oar in his scrawny arms like an imaginary harp, which he stroked with bony fingers. He cackled unpleasantly.

Aidan glanced back along the road, and turned to the ferryman.

'Will you take these others?'

The ferryman nodded.

Aidan looked at Claire.

'I must go back. You cross, while there's still time.'

'*No!*' Claire said vehemently. 'If you stay, you'll die. That'll be it. There must be a way to get across.'

She stared at the ferryman's boat, considering whether the three of them could overpower the old man and row themselves across the bubbling water.

The ferryman eyed her slyly, and took a firmer grip on his oar, as if he could read her thoughts.

'There is another way for you to get back to the other side,' he said, pointing away from the castle along the road beyond the jetty. 'There's a tunnel underneath the river. But you might not like to go that way.'

'Why not? Tell us and we'll go,' Claire said crossly.

'It's not a pleasant way. No one chooses that way.'

'Well, thanks to you we don't have a choice, do we?'

The old man shook his head with a grin.

'No, no choice. Well, go on upstream for half a mile and you'll find the dark entrance to the tunnel set in cliffs beside the road. At first it leads you away from the river, but then it bends back on itself to take you under the waters. But take care. It is not a pleasant way!'

'You've already said that. Goodbye.'

They wasted no more time on talking to the stubborn old man, but hurried on. Soon the road started to rise, running along a narrow shelf between soaring cliffs on one side and a steep drop into the river on the other. They stopped for a moment to rest and looked back the way they had come.

'Look!' Claire said, pointing to the road far away. 'Riders on horseback, coming this way.'

They were only three tiny dots, but moving so fast that they could only have been riders. Aidan nodded grimly.

'They'll be the Reapers, sent after us by the king. If they reach us in the darkness after moonset, we won't be able to leave.'

'Look...' Ben said, pointing to the road nearer to them. 'Isn't there another rider there?'

Sure enough, there was another dot moving fast along the road behind them, a long way ahead of the others, but still too far away from them to make out who – or what – it was.

'Well, whatever's behind us, we can't afford to hang about! Come on!' Claire said.

She and Ben set off, but Aidan continued to stare back along the road. Claire shouted at him in exasperation.

'Aidan! Do you want to get out of here or not?'

He turned, and cycled to catch up with them.

'I'm sorry,' he said. 'I suppose I must escape if I can. But it's like escaping from a wonderful dream. You don't want to wake up.'

'Think of your mother and father in that hospital. Praying that you'll get better. You've *got* to do it, for their sakes!'

'You're right. I know you're right, Claire. I'll try.'

Ben was slightly ahead of them, and called back.

'The tunnel! I can see it!'

Sure enough, just ahead of them was a dark hole in the rocky cliffs. It gaped like a great open mouth, and water drizzled over the entrance from trailing ferns and bushes which overhung the opening like a moustache. It looked far from inviting.

Ben peered into the darkness with a doubtful face.

'What if that old man was tricking us?' he said. 'This looks like the sort of place a monster would live in.'

Claire would have liked to have scoffed at him. But in such a strange world as the Nightland, a monster in a cave would not be out of place. Nonetheless, she assumed a brisk air of certainty.

'Don't be ridiculous, Ben. Why would the ferryman trick us? Come on, let's get on with it!'

They dismounted, and pushed their bikes gingerly forwards into the gloom.

The sound of the river sloshed around inside the rocky walls, so that it was like stepping into the drum of a washing machine. The water slapped and gurgled and

119

groaned in an echoing cacophony of sound. There was a dank musty smell, as if someone had left piles of dirty damp laundry around the place for years. The ground was stony and uneven, and they kept stumbling as they moved further into the darkness. After a hundred metres or so, just as the ferryman had said, there was a bend in the tunnel, and it turned back towards the river, going downwards at quite a steep angle. All of them had lights on their bikes, which they used to pick their way forwards, trying to compromise between the need to hurry, and the danger of slipping on the slimy steep floor. From ahead of them came a deep groaning sound, which must have been some trick of the acoustics of the tunnel, for it sounded like a human groan, except far too deep and loud.

17
The Reapers

'I definitely don't like this!' Ben muttered. 'What's that noise?'

'I don't know,' Claire replied, 'but whatever it is we've got to go on. This is the only way out.'

'We must be right under the river by now!' Aidan said after a few minutes. He took his bicycle light from its bracket on the handlebars and shone it upwards. High above, the little coin of light illuminated a section of the cave ceiling. It glistened, and *moved* slightly. As they stared, some sort of great flapping bird, like a vulture, came thumping through the fetid air and landed on the roof, clinging upside down and pecking furiously at the surface. Eventually it tore a little off and flew away. A glistening smear of red was left behind. The groaning noise grew louder than ever.

'This place is making me feel ill!' Ben said uneasily.

Just then there was a great creaking noise from the darkness off to one side. They swung their lights in that direction and saw what looked like a vast mill wheel turning slowly. Water dripped from its huge spokes. Lashed to the rim of the wheel by great rusty chains was a wraith. He tried helplessly to twist his head towards the light, but he couldn't do it, and was slowly carried upwards and out of sight into the gloom of the upper reaches of the cave, where their bicycle light beams couldn't reach.

'This is a dreadful place. Let's get out of here!' Claire said, and hurried on as fast as she could. But after a few minutes they came to a problem. The floor of the tunnel ahead was flooded. Water dripped from the ceiling, splashing loudly into the pool below, and moisture ran glistening down the slimy walls. Overhead, they could hear the rushing sound of the river, like an endless express train hurtling along.

'Look, there are stepping stones!' Ben said, shining his torch at the pool. It was difficult to judge its depth, because of the way the surface reflected their bicycle lights, but there did seem to be big stones just under the water.

They were hesitating on the brink of the pool when Claire felt something nudging against her ankle. She jumped sideways with a shriek, thinking of rats.

'Ugh! Something touched my leg!'

Aidan shone his light at the ground. Lying on the damp floor of the tunnel was a bone. A long bone that looked like it might have been part of a leg, or an arm, once upon a time.

'Look!'

It was Ben, shining his light further back into the tunnel. On the ground behind them, there were more white bony objects.

'But... they weren't there just now when we walked along that way!' Claire said.

Then they heard a sound. A clattering sound, very faint, as if someone were washing dishes somewhere.

'Look! They're MOVING!'

Aidan and Claire followed Ben's shaking light beam. Further back, the ground was thick with bones, a carpet of bones. And they were shifting, stirring, clunking together. Moving like a nest of worms. As they stared in terror, the bones started to gather into groups, to take shape. Foot bones joined up to leg bones. Skulls attached themselves to spines. Skeletons began to form, and move towards them.

Within seconds they were splashing into the pool ahead, careless of whether it would be shallow or deep. Ben was in the lead.

'There's stones just underneath!' he called. 'It's okay!'

It was hard to carry your bike and keep your balance. Claire shone her light down to pick out a way for her feet. There were round, grey stones down there, just inches below the surface of the pool. They were knobbly with lumps and bumps, and somehow slightly soft, for stones. She stared at the next one she was going to step on, waiting for Ben and Aidan ahead of her to get out of the way. The stone opened eyes and a mouth and looked at her with a look of such misery as she had never seen before. They were heads, these stepping stones! She screamed.

'We're walking on faces! There are people under the water!'

There was no alternative but to go on. It was the most

horrible experience Claire had ever had, treading on all those upturned suffering faces, grey wraith faces forever drowning in that hideous subterranean pool. On the shore behind them the sound of bones knocking and clattering together bounced off the tunnel walls like smashing crockery.

At last they splashed their way through to the other side, and the tunnel began to slope upwards. Another beast-like groan came out of the darkness behind them. Up ahead, the moonlight was beginning to show on the floor and walls, and finally the tunnel led them upwards to the open air.

'I'm glad that's over!' Ben said, breathing deeply.

Claire felt as if she would have liked to soak for hours in a hot bath. The horror of what they'd been through was like something sticking to her skin and making her feel ill. She shuddered as the vulture, or whatever it was, came flapping out of the night and disappeared into the mouth of the tunnel with a squawk, returning to its feast.

They all cycled back along the river to where the road to the jetty came down through the meadows from the courthouse. On the far side of the river they caught their last glimpse of the curmudgeonly old ferryman, whacking at the wraiths who were slow to disembark. There was no sign yet of their pursuers on the road behind, but they all knew that they would gain valuable time on them if the ferryman would carry them across.

Through the meadows, puffing and panting, past the

courthouse, and through the seemingly endless pine woods they cycled. Time was slow and fast at the same time. The pine trees stretched on and on, each exactly the same as its neighbour, so that you felt as if you might be cycling on the spot. But the moon seemed to sink further down each time you looked, as if, like Claire, Aidan and Ben, it was tired and wanted to rest.

By the time they arrived at the fields of corn, the moon was definitely sinking, subsiding sleepily into the bed of the horizon. There was not a second to be lost. The stalks of barley and wheat seemed to watch them as they passed, standing stock still like soldiers on parade, with not a rustle or a whisper of movement. Their three moon shadows fell long on the fields, grim dark companions that stuck to them however fast they went.

They gained the wood, and heard the furious barking of the guardian of the gate. Exhausted, they found that the panic of that chasing noise gave them new desperate energy and when the three-headed beast appeared on the path a long way behind them they were already beyond his reach. He howled forlornly, a chilling sound in the gathering darkness.

Now they were on the final track, lined with great yew trees, which led up to the ridge above the river. They gasped and wheezed as they went up this sloping road, standing on their pedals.

Now they could hear the distant clatter of hoof beats in the wood behind them. Claire called out to Aidan.

'That's them! Come *on*, Aidan! You want to escape, don't you?'

Aidan didn't reply. Claire looked around at him and his face, in spite of the exhausting pace they were keeping up, was as pale as death. Ben was cycling between them. He, on the other hand, was as red in the face as a tomato that might burst at any moment. On his slightly smaller bike, his legs were going round in a blur as the sound of the riders behind sent him into a panic.

'Go, Claire! GO!' he panted.

At last they were on the crest of the ridge. Now there only remained the last downhill swoop to the bridge. Aidan gasped out, 'Wait!' and Claire stopped and turned. He had halted, and was looking backwards. Darkness was flooding across the landscape like a tide of black water, drowning everything in its path. The moon had almost vanished. The last rays of its light glinted on the road leading up to the ridge. Four horseriders were thundering up the slope behind them, only half a mile away now. One of the riders was out in front, and seemed smaller than the others.

Claire grabbed Aidan's handlebars and twisted them around, towards the river. Towards the real world. Already Ben had set off ahead of them, and was gathering speed down the slope towards the bridge, which lay in the murky valley below.

'Aidan! You don't have a choice now! You're fighting for your life. Come!'

126

With a dazed expression, as if in spite of everything his thoughts were elsewhere, Aidan set off, and Claire followed him. They sped faster and faster down the hillside. Ahead, Ben was flying over the hump of the bridge. He, at least, was safe!

Now Claire and Aidan were hurtling past the final corner. Now the bridge was just ahead. The dark water splashed and gurgled, beckoning them to cross. From behind came a desperate call.

'Aidan! Take me with you!'

The cry came from half way down the hillside. Dicie was galloping towards them on a white horse. Its eyes were wild and its mouth and flanks were flecked with foam. Dicie's hair streamed out behind her, her cream gown fluttering like a pennant in the wind.

'Dicie!' Aidan called, squeezing his brakes and skidding dangerously to a halt. Claire braked too, right on the first stone of the bridge.

'She's dead, Aidan!' Claire said. 'She can't cross over. It's too late!'

Then, cresting the ridge behind Dicie, three great black horses stepped onto the horizon, bearing dark hooded figures carrying scythes. It was a sight that sent a shudder down Claire's whole body. For a moment, the moonlight glinted on the wicked curving blades, then, like a candle being extinguished, that final sliver of light vanished, and all was dark. Somewhere far, far away a clock started to strike midnight.

With a rushing sound like a hurricane hurtling

through a forest, the three Reapers bounded forward in the darkness.

'Aidan! Please! Cross the bridge!' Claire pleaded.

Behind her, she heard Ben, now safe on the opposite bank.

'Claire! Cross over!'

Aidan was standing like a statue astride his bike. He looked as if all willpower had seeped out of him, and he might stand there forever. The horses' hooves thundered down the hill. Claire screamed at him, and grabbed his arm.

'Come!'

He didn't move.

In desperation Claire slapped him hard across the cheek.

'Ow! What are you doing!'

'Aidan! Come now! *Please!*'

Shaking his head as if clearing some water out of his ears, he pushed downwards on his pedals and together they travelled the final few metres to cross the bridge. They were safe!

'What did you stop for?' Ben said when they joined him. 'I thought you were just going to stay there until you got caught!'

Out of the darkness on the other side of the river, Dicie appeared on her horse. She looked across the bridge in their direction, but it seemed that she couldn't see them.

'Aidan! Are you there?' she called. Her voice was faint. Too faint for the few metres that separated them.

'I'm here, Dicie!' Aidan called back. 'Cross over!'

'I can't see what's ahead, Aidan! It's just like a fog. Are you through there, in the mist?'

'There's a bridge. Right in front of you. Cross over!'

'Aidan . . . ' Claire started.

'I'll come to the middle of the bridge. I'll meet you.'

Before Claire could stop him, Aidan dismounted from his bike and strode to the middle of the bridge.

Now Dicie started to urge her horse forward.

The three Reapers arrived. But instead of following Dicie, they reined in their horses and watched.

As Dicie's horse stepped on the bridge, a sound like a wind hurrying millions of brittle autumn leaves sprang up from nowhere. As Claire watched in horror, the horse, and Dicie herself, seemed to grow transparent. Their flesh became a faint white mist that blew away from the skeletons beneath. Dicie's pretty face and smooth limbs all but vanished, and a skeleton child on a skeleton horse halted on the bridge, only a metre away from where Aidan stood with outstretched hand.

A voice, that sounded like Dicie's, but came from the air all around them, spoke.

'I can't. I can't leave, can I, Aidan?'

Aidan's face was wet with tears, and his lips trembled. He shook his head.

'I can't see you, Aidan. But I know you're there. Goodbye! Remember me!'

And Dicie urged her horse around, and walked it back to where the Reapers waited in silence. As she retreated, both the horse and herself regained their form. Finally, she turned in her saddle, and her sweet face was radiant with a smile.

'Farewell, Aidan! Remember the Nightland! Remember me!'

And then Dicie and the Reapers walked their horses away into the darkness.

18
A Mystery for the Watchman

Roddy Simpson, the night security man at Southlands Hospital, liked to have a little drink of whisky to warm him up before patrolling the hospital grounds and outlying buildings. It was a large site, and took at least an hour to patrol thoroughly. So a little sip of whisky from the bottle in his office desk, supplemented by a few more little sips from the hip flask in his pocket as he made his rounds, was a great comfort on a cold misty night like tonight.

It was because of the warming effect of the whisky, perhaps, that he didn't quite know whether or not to trust his eyes when he saw what looked like a patient, a young boy in pyjamas, clambering out of the window of one of the wards and running across the wet grass into the darkness.

'Oi!' Roddy called out, and lumbered as fast as his eighteen stone would let him towards the vanishing figure. This wasn't a prison, of course, but it was still a little irregular for patients to go shooting off in the middle of the night! Surely there must be some forms to be signed, at least?

He got half way across the grassy field before he caught sight of the boy again. But now, instead of wearing pyjamas, the boy was clad in jeans and a fleece, and sitting astride a bicycle!

'Oi!' Roddy called out again, in a faltering way. Surely it was the same boy, tallish, with wavy blond hair?

But the boy didn't heed his call. He pedalled away into the night, in the direction of the Archersfield gate, and Roddy went back to his patrol, shaking his head as if he'd seen a ghost.

When one of the nurses told him, the next day, about the coma patient who had apparently woken up and made their own way home in the middle of the night, he didn't say what he'd seen. After all, he should perhaps have reported it at the time. Also, surely, he must have been mistaken about the bicycle. He decided that he would cut down, just a little, on the whisky in future. In a lonely night-time job like this, you couldn't let your imagination go running away with you, or who knew where you'd end up?

More Fiction for you to enjoy

The Midnight Clowns

by Roberts Dodds

In the middle of the night, you hear feet on the stairs. They make a sound like wet fish being slapped onto a slab. They must be very big feet. And they're coming closer . . . What would you do if a sinister troupe of supernatural clowns had picked you out as their next victim? That's the terrifying plight that faces Ben Swift and his sister Claire. If they can't find a way to outwit their pursuers, Ben will be forced to drink the clowns' magic blue potion – with terrible consequences!

'**A thoroughly spine-chilling thriller, lightened by the realistic and often very funny exchanges.**' *Shelf Life,* Scottish Book Trust

ISBN 0862649935 £3.99

More Fiction for you to enjoy

Wings To Fly

by

PATRICK COOPER

*I couldn't stop thinking about the Birdman, and that story he'd
told me. It got mixed up inside me with the talk of the war
and my mother's crying, and I had nightmares of screaming
aeroplanes and charred hands and black, broken faces.*

Sarah was thirteen when she met Julian, the Birdman.
He told her about the Great War – about flying and
fighting in the skies over France, about being
wounded, and the death of his friend Harry. She was
strangely drawn to him in this time of tumultuous
change, a time of danger and loss, a time of growing
up and of finding the wings to fly . . .

'A subtly poignant book' *achuka.co.uk*

**'A moving story of love, loss and the
devastating effects of war'** *Financial Times*

ISBN 184270026X £4.99

More Fiction for you to enjoy

RIVER of SECRETS

by Griselda Gifford

Fran is very upset because her mother has remarried
and she has to live with her stepfather and his son
at her gran's old home. She was very fond of her
gran, who has recently been found dead in the
nearby river. Was her death an accident? Fran is
sure someone is to blame and she's determined to
solve the mystery. Is the weird girl, Fay, who lives
next door, hiding something? And why does
another new friend, Denny, warn her against Fay's
strange magic? Fran faces danger when the river
almost claims a new victim, before she finally
unlocks its secrets in a surprising and exciting
climax to the story.

'A nail-biting novel' 4 star review, *Mizz Magazine*

ISBN 1842700456 £4.99

More Fiction for you to enjoy

The FIRING

by Richard MacSween

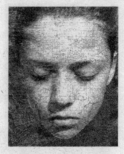

Stuck in a poxy village where nothing happens
Anna has to ask herself what she's done wrong?
Having to share living space with a useless
stepfather. And don't even mention those twins.

Things can only get better when a stranger arrives.
Two strangers – there's a son as well. And his stupid
name is only the first mystery about him.

**'A cracking first novel – sharp, funny and
authentic yet haunted by the strange magic
of a fairy tale. Anna is a teenage heroine for
our time.'** Blake Morrison

'An exceptional first novel.' Melvin Burgess

ISBN 1842700553 £4.99

More Fiction for you to enjoy

CRAZY GAMES

by

SANDRA GLOVER

'What you doing, Col?' Brad had asked.
'Sharpening this,' Colford had answered as if sitting around,
in a World War 1 uniform, sharpening a piece of wood with a
rather evil-looking knife, was perfectly reasonable behaviour.

The last thing Brad wants to encourage is the
friendship of Colford Rattersby, a strange boy who
talks to statues and who seems to live in a fantasy
world because the real one is so awful.
But, despite having plenty of problems of his own,
not least his relationship with fiery Stacey, Brad gets
drawn into Colford's increasingly bizarre behaviour
and the games which are starting to drift from
harmless fantasy towards dangerous reality . . .

ISBN 1842700669 £9.99 (hbk)